Arabs

DOWN UNDER

Arabs

DOWN UNDER

Mohammed Mahfoodh Al Ardhi

South Street Press

ARABS DOWN UNDER

Published by
South Street Press
8 Southern Court
South Street
Reading
Berkshire
RG1 4QS
UK
www.southstreetpress.co.uk

South Street Press is an imprint of Garnet Publishing Limited

Copyright © Mohammed Mahfoodh Al Ardhi 2008

First Edition

ISBN 13: 978-1-902932-19-4

British Library Cataloguing-in-Publication Data
A catalogue record for this book is available from the British Library

Typeset by PHi, India
Jacket design by David Rose
Cover illustration used with permission of Stephen Finn/Fotolia.com

Printed by Biddles, UK

Contents

Prologue   vii

1   Queenstown – Extremism and Fundamentalism   1

2   Lake Wakatipu – Nationalism and Democracy   7

3   Milford Sound – Arab and Israeli Relations   13

4   Mount Cook – Women and Marriage   23

5   Christchurch – Islam in Daily Life   31

6   Marlborough – Arab and Western Alliances   37

7   Wellington – Democracy Examined   43

8   Rotorua – Westerners in Arabia   53

9   Waitomo Caves – Oil and New Zealand Horses   61

10   Auckland – Arabs in Western Universities   67

11   Reflections   77

Epilogue   85

Prologue

'Go in quest of knowledge even unto China.'
'An hour's contemplation is better than a year's adoration.'
'Who so honoureth the learned, honoureth me.'
'Seek knowledge from the cradle to the grave.'
'One learned man is harder on the devil than a
thousand ignorant worshippers.'
'The ink of the scholar is more holy than the blood of the martyr.'
'He who leaveth home in search of knowledge
walketh in the path of God.'

The Prophet Mohammed

It was not 'unto China' but New Zealand that Ibrahim took his family. It was in the New Zealand winter, July 2007 that he chose to take a break from the excessive summer heat of his home in the Middle East. He had been contemplating making a trip 'Down Under' for many years but the pressure of life and the growing up of his family had denied him that opportunity until now. It was hot in Europe with heavier than usual rains and flooding in the United Kingdom so it was a logical choice to travel to the Southern, rather than remain in the Northern Hemisphere, besides which, he had an old friend, Mark, in New Zealand whom he had not met in many years. This was as good a time as any to reacquaint himself and retrace those intervening years of absence.

Ibrahim was a freelance journalist covering much of the background to the geopolitical situation in the Middle East and much of his investigative reporting had centred upon the fractured peace and political turmoil in Iraq. He had been well educated as a lad as his father had sent him to England for all his secondary education and to the United States to complete his university qualifications in journalism. That was many years ago; he was now in his mid-forties and channelling his own children through their advanced schooling years. He had two sons and three daughters.

It was of increasing concern to him that with all the anti-Israeli and anti-American ill-feeling among his Arab nationals, the tarnished image of his people was beginning to stick very firmly and unfavourably in the psyche of the West. It was unjustifiable, in his view, that his children were growing up in a world which did not respect the Arab, his religion or his culture. In fact, Western public opinion was now so generally opposed to the activities of political extremists across the globe, regardless of their ethnicity or political agenda, that the whole of the Arab race was immediately being put under the microscope, indeed many in the West had become totally paranoid. Was he, as a dedicated Muslim and responsible father, going to stand by and watch the insidious psychological destruction and malignity of his people?

Mark, his old friend in New Zealand, was a true Englishman. He was a steadfast Anglican and loyalist supporter of the British monarchy. At the age of about 18, Mark had thought to follow his father and train to become a clergyman. However, upon the best counselling of the day, he was advised to complete his studies in English and the Arts and travel the world. At 19 he began to implement that advice; he migrated of his own choice to New Zealand, leaving behind in England the whole of his family, to start a life anew in a former colonial outpost the other side of the world. Mark was now 66 and retired. Having travelled the world extensively as a highly skilled journalist and correspondent for a leading news agency, he had never married but retained his commitment to his faith. Education, journalism and travel had been the combined catalyst that had brought Ibrahim and Mark together as colleagues thirty years earlier and their friendship had stood the test of time since. They were on an intellectual plateau of understanding that permitted an uninhibited freedom of thought and speech that was seemingly only enjoyed by those who had lived a life among the global community. Certainly both shared the view that many of those less fortunate themselves, through a lack of education and life experience, had built up within themselves mental walls of prejudice so impenetrable that even faced with the truth their bias presented immovable barriers of ignorance and indifference. To heal the wounds of the past and plan for the future, hope remained in the wider education of the youth of the present.

1

Queenstown – Extremism and Fundamentalism

It was −18°C in the region. Storms and sleet-bearing clouds, then periodic falls of snow had blocked roads, stranded vehicles and holiday-makers, brought down power lines, temporarily closed the airport and finally had forced the postponement of the Winter Festival. Within a week of this, a large anti-cyclone had drifted across the Tasman Sea and embraced the whole of the South Island of New Zealand. The isobars had become wider, the winds had dropped, the lingering cloud had vanished and brilliant sunshine had appeared to the joy of all. With mid-day temperatures now stable at about +4°C, the flight touched down at 1500hrs, right on schedule, at Queenstown. It was Saturday, 7th July 2007, in the middle of the antipodean winter.

Disembarking was a closely knit Muslim family of seven, from the Arabian Peninsula. Temperatures in their homeland of the Middle East were about +40°C, a far cry from those they experienced now. As they emerged from within the Terminal they were clearly well prepared as layer upon layer of thick clothing, plus their traditional wear, was all too obvious and, needless to say, necessary. However, the glorious sunshine which prevailed not only would have given them the finest alpine views of the Southern Alps of New Zealand on descent but also softened the blow of reality, of extreme cold, that soon would follow.

"Ibrahim, how wonderful to see you again: welcome to New Zealand!"

"We are delighted to be here, Mark, after all these years. Let me introduce the family: my wife, Mona; my oldest lad, 17, Khamis; my youngest son, 13, Juma; my oldest daughter, Zamzam; then Rabab; and lastly my youngest, Farah." They all smiled excitedly with the joy of once again being on firm ground, stretching their legs and breathing the fresh air of a completely new country with new people.

"Well I am delighted to have you all here safe and sound. You do realise, I hope, that you have arrived at the last bus stop on the planet?"

With the pleasantries over, two Toyota 4WD Prado vehicles, equipped with tyre chains and roof-mounted storage boxes, were signed over to Ibrahim by Tony and Helen, the young proprietors of a small overland 4WD rental company based in Christchurch. As it was the last fortnight of the winter school holidays in New Zealand it had been necessary to source these vehicles in Christchurch and pre-position them in Queenstown. All 4WD rental vehicles locally were fully committed with families and an active skiing season that was well underway. Certainly it was absolutely essential, at this time of the year, to have 4WD capability with snow and ice an every day feature on the roads. Coupled with this factor, Ibrahim and Mark would be doing all the driving and a preference for larger vehicles was thought desirable for the group. Once settled into their hotel, in the heart of the town, in Duke Street, it was possible to begin planning the programme of their intended stay of some 17 days which would see them finally depart from Auckland at the top of the North Island. It was to be an action packed, totally comprehensive but enjoyable break for everyone. Above all it was to be that rare opportunity to re-energise mind, body and soul in the crystal clear air of this unique and somewhat isolated island nation in the South West Pacific Ocean.

"Ibby," Mark, now relaxed, reverted to Ibrahim's nick-name of old, "you are just so fortunate to arrive here in such fantastic weather. Surely this good fortune must be the hand of Providence?"

"You mean the hand of Allah?"

"Of course, Ibby: what is more wonderful is that the weather forecast for at least the next two weeks will bring more of the same; it is indeed a generous 'hand' and definitely very welcome. I don't want to be driving on black ice! That is the ice you cannot see. It will be melted by about 10 o'clock each morning. We need to be off the roads by 4 as the ice will reform smartly after the sun disappears."

"Yes, have no worries, Mark. We will keep to short days on the road whenever possible. Now I have been thinking of our options for the next few days while we are here. We will reserve a whole day, as you suggest, to make the round trip to Milford Sound if road conditions permit but what young Juma and some of the girls really want to do right now is to test their skills on the snow slopes."

"We have six great ski-fields in close proximity to Queenstown, Ibby. Some of the best skiers come from all over the world to be here. Apart from our Australian skiers, who seem to take up permanent winter residence here, we do attract those enthusiasts from the northern hemisphere who just cannot get enough of our winter skiing. I was delighted to learn that you will be getting young Khamis to undertake his tertiary education in Toronto. We have many Canadians here right now, also skiing."

"Yes, we thought that a Canadian education would broaden his mind and give him some mental independence from the colleges and universities in the United States or Europe. It will be very interesting to see how he develops. So where are your ski fields, exactly?"

"Perhaps firstly, Coronet Peak; I personally recommend this one as it is just a 20 minute drive away. It has the advantage of exceptionally commanding alpine views of the whole of the Queenstown area with a backdrop of the Remarkables to be seen in the distance and Lake Wakatipu in the foreground. Then the Remarkables itself has a good ski field with Cardrona, Treble Cone, Snow Park, and Waiorau Snow Farm making up the others; they are all excellent."

"We will opt for Coronet Peak, Mark."

So it was, on the first available day, the family moved off in the two vehicles to Coronet Peak. The older lad, Khamis, and two of the girls joined Mark in one vehicle and the others remained with Ibby. As Mark had not been to Queenstown for many years, the very years he was covering news stories for his news agency in Europe and the Middle and Far East, Khamis was put to the test on day one in this, a foreign country where driving was on the opposite side of the road to which he was accustomed; he became the 'navigator'. He was too young to be 'co-driver' but if he was given the chance, which legally he could not be, he would have been behind the wheel in an instant! Such is youth. With the tracery of roads, rivers and ranges of mountains reduced to scale in maps on his lap, the environment around him had come to life. This little activity each day thereafter became the 'norm' for the whole of the journey. After all, Mark was retired and two heads were definitely better than one and certainly, when one of the heads was a very talented and bright 17 year old, the route finding was going to be simplified, surely? With the daily routine established, Khamis silently slipped a CD into the dash-board music system and within seconds the soft tones of a recital from the Qur'an drifted through the cabin.

"Mark, you don't think we are all terrorists do you?" It was an alarmingly straightforward question put directly with the concerned innocence of youth.

"Khamis, if I thought you were a terrorist I wouldn't be sitting beside you now, would I?"

"No, I guess not, but the whole world thinks we are terrorists," he pleaded.

"If you were in a taxi," began Mark slowly, "driving around Manhattan and you saw a green man on the corner, then turned into another street and saw another green man, then one more on another footpath, would you conclude that the whole of Manhattan was full of green men?"

Khamis thought. "No, of course not! I have only seen three green men."

"Then, if you hear of only three terrorist attacks, then the whole world is not full of terrorists, is it? You can only account for three, not millions."

"Yes, but … …,"

"I know your concerns, Khamis. Now let me be more specific. When I was your age, during the pre-Israel era, we feared the cruelty and cunning of the Irgun and Haganah. These were Jewish guerrilla movements; terrorists in fact. Now you personally know and hear of Hamas and Fatah. Both these began as anti-Israeli guerrilla organizations, terrorists, but of very recent times they have matured somewhat and taken on much more of a political role. Essentially, Khamis, terrorism is the systematic and organised use of violence and intimidation to force a government to buckle under pressure and accept certain demands."

"So why do we have names like 'extremist' and 'militant'; are these the same as terrorists?"

"Essentially, yes. Just like tea has many flavours, tea is tea! In the press we use a number of words to give the emphasis we need in describing an event. When you look at a news-clip on Al-Jazeera you don't split hairs on the categorisation or definition of an individual. You look at the damage that has been done, and then label the perpetrator! Followers of Al-Qaeda were seen initially as 'extremists' but soon we reshaped our thinking and saw them as the deadly global 'terrorist' organisation. Following the 11th September attacks of 2001, you will recall the bomb attack on the *USS Cole*, the blasts in Tunis, Bali, Mombassa, Riyadh, Casablanca, Istanbul and Madrid. The list goes on with bombings in London and the failed car bombs in London and Glasgow. We attribute all of these, rightly or wrongly, to Al-Qaeda."

"Our Islamic belief also denounces all forms of terrorism, Mark."

"Yes, I appreciate that and also there is no place in your Islamic society for suicide bombers as well."

"I understand why we have suicide bombers, Mark. They are 'extremists' in the full sense of the word. I know their behaviour too stems almost invariably from desperation and a sense of hopelessness in their cause. They are emotionally, and often in revenge, driven to do what they do." Khamis paused thoughtfully and continued, "Yes, Mark, I agree, there is no place for this in our Islam. What I cannot understand is what you call *fundamentalism?*"

"Well, for a moment think of the Taliban then we can put a face on who are the fundamentalists. The Taliban are unremittingly *fundamentalists*. These people have a strict interpretation, in their view, of the literal meaning of your Qur'an. However, the very word *Taliban* means *students* and this was the name given to a handful of young lads who were sickened by the excesses of their local warlords in Afghanistan. They were never accepted by mainstream Muslims as their understanding was never of the traditional Islamic values."

"Ah, now this is becoming clearer."

After a few moments in silence and deep thought, Mark responded: "Simply put, Khamis, fundamentalism is the unquestioning faith in your traditional Islamic teachings but more importantly, this must be seen to be coupled with a dynamic political force."

"I see!"

"What you will be interested to know my young Khamis is that 'fundamentalism' has just as many roots in Christianity as it does in Islam."

"I didn't know that!"

"Few do; let me briefly explain."

Mark went on again, slowly, but methodically to outline to Khamis that a religious movement arose in the USA about 1919 which opposed all theories of evolution and anthropology, teaching that God transcends all the laws of nature, and that He manifests Himself by exceptional and extraordinary activities. Belief in the literal meaning of the Scriptures was an essential tenet. Mark also recalled that in 1925 a professor of science was convicted of violating the State laws of Tennessee by teaching evolution, and the incident aroused interest and controversy far beyond the religious circles of the USA.

"Now what I would like you to do, Khamis is talk to your father and come up with what you understand to be the list of fundamentals of your Islamic faith. Do you think you could do that for me?"

"Yes, sure."

With that thought spinning around in his head, it was a quiet Khamis who began the day. In fact he opted not to join his younger brother and sisters who were determined to get the best out of the snow conditions and the planned skiing activities, albeit this adventure was completely new to them.

It had been a successful day with twists and tumbles in the snow coupled with some spirited sessions with the ski instructor. Although completely alien a sport, it was important that they were exposed to this activity if for no other reason than they could speak knowledgably one day to their friends in the West. As for Khamis, he did speak to his father and as he made ready for bed he drew out a pencil and pad and wrote down the fundamentals of his faith. These emerged as the Five Pillars of Islam: the belief of *shahada,* that there is no other God but Allah and that Mohammed was his Prophet; prayer; fasting; almsgiving; and the Hajj – the pilgrimage to Mecca. He also wrote down the six articles of his faith, *iman:* belief in Allah; His messengers like Moses, Jesus and Mohammed; Holy books; angels; the Day of Judgement and Destiny. He was determined to rush to Mark and tell him in the morning!

2

Lake Wakatipu – Nationalism and Democracy

"It is our second largest lake in the South Island. Our largest you will see tomorrow when we head off to Milford Sound."

Mark was speaking to the family as they stood and absorbed spectacular and breathtaking, endless views of the lake. Spell-bound, silent and even semi-stunned by their view of Lake Wakatipu and its surrounding mountains and valleys beneath, they snapped away with their cameras. They were on the Look Out veranda outside the top of the Skyline Gondola which had vertically transported them into this almost entirely new world; a world above the busy streets of Queenstown below.

"There are various apocryphal accounts of how the town was named," continued Mark. "The most popular suggestion was that a local gold digger exclaimed that the town was fit for Queen Victoria; hence Queenstown. With all the noise from the bars and pubs, last night, however, you probably think the place is the Las Vegas of New Zealand, some indeed have called this beautiful spot, the *Vegas by the Lake*."

"Clearly they had a perceived fixation on the commerce-oriented tourism the town now exudes," added Ibrahim somewhat cynically.

"Our adventure sports," Mark rejoined quickly, "as you have seen make this, certainly, a natural focal point for our healthy and affluent youth. No-one is poor down there in the town. With the Arctic temperatures today the youngsters literally can be *cool* and properly *chill out!* Our Maoris have a more interesting opinion as to the naming of the lake. They believe the word *Waka* means 'trough' or lake, and *tipu* means 'goblin' or 'monster'. So when the monster breathes we get the regular rise and fall of the fresh water!"

"So you have your own Loch Ness Monster," exclaimed Juma joyfully.

"Well we certainly have our fair share of Scots here Juma, I grant you that. In fact I have Scottish blood in my veins and I will show you the family tartan when you reach my home in a few days' time."

Turning to Ibrahim, Mark quietly reflected upon a visit he once made to Turkey. "Mentioning Queen Victoria a moment ago, Ibby, did you ever see that wonderful chandelier that the Queen presented to the last of the Sultans of the Ottomans before the Empire collapsed at the close of the First World War?"

"The one in the Dolma Bahce Palace in Istanbul, beside the Bosporus?"

"Yes. I have vivid memories of that great city; its unique succession of over a thousand mosques with their perfectly proportioned domes punctuated by minarets – what a great sight."

"Ah, colonialism and the World Wars fractured hopes of a restoration of Arab nationalism, the concept of which sought a union of Arab countries. Arab nationalism also, Mark, tends to be secular, like the Ba'ath Party in Syria and of Saddam in Iraq. Revival of our classical Islamic institution of government, the Caliphate, is a religious concept and the view, I might add, Mark, largely of the minority extremists like Al-Qaeda. What we must not do, Mark is confuse the two concepts!"

"Yes, the distinction between the two concepts is one lost on most Western minds! But they were great days, Ibby, of which you can well be proud. Not only did the Ottoman Empire collapse but we then saw the birth of the new and independent states within your Gulf region."

"Yes. Many people to this day do not appreciate that Iraq did not exist at all at the beginning of the 20th century so the 'nationalism' to which you refer can only now be rebuilt within the bounds of each new state. Sadly, Arab nationalism, as a single entity across the region, will unlikely ever be seen again."

"Talking of Iraq for a second, Ibby," Marked pressed curiously, "do you see a development in line with that of the secular state of Turkey?"

"You mean, post the withdrawal of all US and Coalition troops?"

"Yes."

"Erdogan continues to do a magnificent job in leading his party of moderate Islamists. His Justice and Development Party (AKP) has brought years of economic prosperity and political calm to Turkey. The AKP has combined free-market economic policies with generous social benefits for the poor. The nation needs to thank him! You know, Mark, not only does Turkey sit on a doorstep to the West, indeed with one foot in the West and the other in the East with the Bosporus between the legs, but Turkey also sits on a time bomb! Will his Turkey, I ask myself, ever see full democracy or return to an era of weak coalitions dominated by the Army? It took Kemal Ataturk, you know, all his whole life to build up and keep the state secular. I wish them all the luck that they can get in their domestic reforms and application to join the European Union. It is about time that new blood was injected into Europe to stem the tide of moral bankruptcy which prevails in pockets of some of the member states of the Union."

"So, are you saying that we cannot expect to see the Turkish solution of a secular state being applied in Iraq?"

"I sometimes wonder if anyone ever reads their history books," exclaimed an enthused Ibrahim. "You may remember when Faisal was crowned king of the then newly-created country of Iraq in 1921, that the British engineered a democratic scheme loosely based on their British constitutional monarchy. It was a complete failure and by the time of its collapse in 1958, Iraqis had been subjected to the rule of no less than 50 cabinets! Doesn't this ring true today?"

"So looking to the future, Ibby, 10, 20, perhaps 50 years ahead what can you see for Iraq?"

"Well if we actually begin to learn from history, Mark, not the Turkish, nor the British, nor the American systems will work in Iraq. Appointments like an 'Envoy to the Middle East' is just another example of the intransigence and head-in-the-sand attitude we now see from the West, towards attempting to meet the genuine needs of the people of Iraq."

"Will the endemic lawlessness ever end, I wonder," muttered a puzzled Mark.

"Mark, what we have beyond the criminal element which is bent on thwarting any action to bring law and order, is a continuing trend of sectarian violence. First and foremost, this has to stop! With the fall of Saddam, in the vacuum which followed, we have seen an ideological adjustment which has given the Shi'a Muslims breathing space they never enjoyed before. We now have a clash between our Sunni and Shi'a communities, and other minor sects, on an unprecedented scale. As you know, Iraq has an overwhelming majority of Shi'a Muslims and this pattern is not only permanent but efforts to change it would be heinous. We therefore must find a solution recognising this religiously demo-graphic reality."

"So would you look towards the Iranian solution?"

"God forbid, Mark! I think I would commit Japanese hari-kari before I would ever suggest a Shi'a, Persian, Iranian solution to satisfy a Sunni, Arabian, Iraqi problem!"

"But there must be some parallels, surely?"

"Yes, there are. As with many communities, the people of Iran consider it an expression of their religion to contribute positively to the political process. In fact there has been a significant measure of dissent within the ranks of the Iranian hierarchal structure in the past. You may remember in the 1990s, one Kadivar argued that Iran could not have clerical rule and claim to be a democracy at the same time. He was jailed of course and reaffirmed his view that the Revolution was being superseded by a new clerical despotism. Then Khomeini's designated successor, the Grand Ayatollah Ali Montazeri, came out in support of Kadivar, when complaining about the mass execution of political prisoners post their war with Iraq, claiming that what was being practised in Iran was not Islam. Voices from the seminary at Qom, the Vatican of the Shi'a sect, have long been voluble and have in fact forced change."

"Of their organization, Ibby, how do you see any similar approach for a future Iraq?"

"Mark, I have visited Iran and spoken with some of their leaders; I know the Iranians."

"Yes, and did you get any feel for their inner feelings?"

"It is very difficult to see through the Iranian fog as they have a population of 71 million with a multitude of languages and ethnicities. Although it has elements of democracy, including an elected president and parliament, the State is finally governed by a handful of individuals. Components like the Revolutionary Guards, the Council of Guardians, the judiciary, the senior clerics of whom almost all are strictly conservative, and the vast administrative machine which reports directly to the supreme leader all influence the direction of Iran. The Council of Guardians attempts to operate in a similar way to the US Senate or the UK House of Lords, conceptually an Upper House, but without the democratic content and overview. Even within these non-elected bodies corruption and nepotism are rampant; we will never know to what lengths their internal systems penetrate society."

"If the non-elected elements were replaced with supervised, elected posts, would that be a guide to Iraq?"

"Probably, Mark. Absolute transparency is needed these days in government for credibility to be achieved globally. Iraq, I believe, will finally become a fully, democratically elected, one-party state; a Shi'a state. Or, if not this, it will split into two states; Shi'a and Sunni with the Kurds in the Sunni state. In any event the people will formulate this development, not the USA, Britain or the United Nations!"

"Yes, Ibby. In Latin we would say: *vox populi vox Dei*; which literally means, the voice of the People is the voice of God!"

It was very refreshing and intellectually heartening and stimulating for both Mark and Ibrahim to get together after all these years and although one was twenty years the senior of the other their professional discipline, within the industry of journalists and writers, gave them a unique quality and mutual ability to discuss topics without personal constraint or inhibition. So it was as they stood overlooking Lake Wakatipu.

♣　♣　♣　♣

"We are going on the Luge," offered the quietly spoken young Juma with more than a measure of uncontrollable excitement in his voice. The Luge was a self-styled race down the hillside within a narrow channel seated in what appeared to be a plastic bucket with handle bars, perhaps more accurately imagined as a sled or toboggan! Off they went, sliding feet first down a steeply curved bank and seemingly endless track; two lads and three lasses! Recovering from the event Khamis complained bitterly as his legs were too big and the breaking mechanism fell considerably short of what he thought was a minimum.

"We had to steer by shifting our weight from side to side and the handle bars were supposed to be a break but I couldn't hold the run-away horse! Just look at my hands!" Indeed they were ice blue with the cold.

"So you don't think you want to enter in the next Winter Olympics in the European Alps, Khamis?" Ibrahim was smiling as he said it but was not in the slightest bit sympathetic! Such was the joy of parenthood.

"Well the last item, apart from shopping, on the agenda for today is a trip on the old steam boat down there." Mark pointed to the SS *Earnslaw* docked beside the jetty in the heart of the town itself. The SS *Earnslaw* was indeed a vintage, coal-fired steam ship and had been plying the lake ferrying fuel, supplies, people and the livestock of deer, Scottish highland cattle and sheep, to the small settlements of Kingston,

Glenorchy and Kinloch and farms, like the Walter Peak High Country Hill Farm, situated around the lake, since 1912. The ship's name came from Mount Earnslaw, the highest of the surrounding peaks, near the head of the lake overlooking the hamlet of Glenorchy.

It took some time to ride the return trip of the Gondola and actually get to the jetty. In fact the family nearly missed the last sailing of the day at 4 in the afternoon bound toward the Walter Peak High Country Hill Farm. This 'station', as it more accurately was called, was developed like so many of New Zealand's early properties by a pioneering Scottish family. Today the station mirrored much of its original setting but had moved forward with the times and operated both as a profitable company with a mixed farming operation and a tourist attraction. With the sun setting and only tourists to be picked up for their return to Queenstown, the skipper was not wasting any time. He wanted to be berthed once again in daylight in the town.

A walk about the decks of the old stoker revealed a comprehensive set of photos and documented history of the *Earnslaw* in the Fo'c'sle Gallery. Here was the real story of the 'Lady of the Lake'. Ibrahim and Mark reminisced over the gunwale of the stern lower deck, braced against the chill wind with their kapok and down jackets, while the family joined the rest of the tourist passengers snugly seated in the upper saloon warmed by the steam-generated heaters. As to what happened there in those minutes just prior to return would be an occurrence the younger members of the family would never ever forget. The ship's pianist had gathered the visitors before her and over a printed song sheet they all sang in unison; all, that is, including Arabs, Japanese, Dutch, French, Norwegian and Chinese travellers. It was a mini-United Nations! Most interesting of all was the revelation that Ibrahim's daughter, Rabab, was invited at one point to play the piano whereupon she excelled herself with a rendition of her State's national anthem. As the ship docked they all rather fittingly sang 'Auld Lang Syne', a tribute surely to the early settlers of the lake and their new found global camaraderie. This real feeling of friendship among the youth, regardless of colour, race or creed, was indicative of the birth of a new era. Here was witnessed the encroachment of Western, Middle Eastern and Oriental ideas with new consumer habits, such as satellite television, into modern society. Here was the tangible rise of a generation that had no direct memory of either Osama bin Laden, revolution or war.

3

Milford Sound – Arab and Israeli Relations

"All the Muslim countries voted against the formation of the State of Israel in 1948, Ibby, and even Britain abstained." Mark was explaining how the Palestinian problem first emerged. "After the close of World War II, Ibby, my country of England was exhausted and almost bankrupt with fighting off Hitler. I was just 7 years old at the time and my father had only just returned from the battle fields of North Africa."

"So who made the decision to form the State of Israel in 1948?" enquired a puzzled Ibrahim cautiously.

"Ibby, Britain handed over the problem of Palestine to the then newly formed United Nations and a UN Special Committee on Palestine (UNSCOP) suggested that separate Jewish and Arab states be formed and united in an economic union, with Jerusalem and its environs placed under international control. This was passed by the UN General Assembly at the end of 1947. All the Arab nations opposed the decision. Immediately thereafter, Britain ended its mandate in Palestine."

"Now, I remember," Ibrahim warmed to the discussion, "that Israeli military mastermind Ben Gurion, moved in with his Haganah forces and his Irgun and Stern Gang terrorists and trampled all over the Palestinians."

"In short, yes, Ibby."

"And the Arab-Israeli wars of 1956 and 1967 were simply an extension of Ben Gurion's earlier conflict?"

"Yes," nodded a saddened Mark, "and what is more disconcerting is that the UN Resolution 242, of 1967, did absolutely nothing for the Palestinians who became divided by exile, were crowded into refugee camps and began a stateless life in what our world has heard about all too often as the Occupied Territories."

"So Israel was a State created by war and preserved by war?"

"Yes, Ibby." Mark became solemn and deeply thoughtful then added:

"By that eventful year of 1967, Israel was more of an outpost of the West. I want you to understand, Ibby, it was the US, France and West Germany that sustained, armed and guarded Israel."

"And today, Mark," viewed a more satisfied Ibrahim, "we see that the Jewish lobby in both Republican and Democrat camps firmly ties one arm behind the back of their President, whomever he may be! American foreign policy is not only substantially flawed, Mark, it is compromised by the Jewish Lobby!"

"Let's be more specific, Ibby! American foreign policy in respect of the Palestinian Arabs has failed!" exclaimed an aggrieved Mark, "we cannot rely on a biased viewpoint from the US any longer if we want to see change for the Palestinian Arabs. Apart from the fact that we now have, geographically, a state within a state we still have the question of the guardianship of the holy shrines."

"The plight of Palestinian Arabs is such that only Arabs will be able to resolve the way forward. With a much more accountable United Nations these days, than formerly in say 1948, there is hope that new initiatives to the UN General Assembly from the Arabs themselves will not fall on barren land. It is certain that any US pro-Israeli position would have to be isolated. With the US right of veto, this obstacle would generate new challenges for us all. A new beam of light and a new strategy to overcome the plight of the Palestinian Arabs is something the world must come to acknowledge and accept if we were going to halt extremism."

It was a salutary beginning to a beautiful day, but cold, as Mark and Ibrahim reflected upon the Arab/Israeli situation. It was not a feeling of hate or disrespect for Judaism that they had, nor indeed any Arab had for their religion, but it was a manifestation of concern and criticism of Israeli current policy. After all, elsewhere in the modern world, walls and barriers were being knocked down not built up!

"Ibby, I am confident that we do have better times ahead. The Bush-Blair romance is long over and now Anglo-American politics are back on a new footing and refocused. In Washington there is a new team gradually replacing the neocon and in Britain we are not hampered with a Jewish lobby and indeed, quite the opposite, we have a large Arab and pro-Arab population. It could well be, after all these years since 1948, that your old ally of Britain may well reappear to help fight the diplomatic battles in the UN General Assembly?"

"Well I sincerely hope so, Mark. I would love to see the long calcified peace process revitalised and turned around in my lifetime." It was on this sober note that Ibrahim began to smile for the first time that day but just as Mark had thought the topic had come to a natural conclusion, Ibby, re-opened the discussion: "Mark, just how strong is the Israeli case to reoccupy or command world opinion in their favour?"

Mark reflected thoughtfully. "If you were a north-countryman in England, Ibby, they would attempt to reply with an old saying: 'the answer lies in the soil!' And, it may well be that the answer does lay in the soil."

A puzzled Ibrahim reflected upon this unusual response from Mark, rather despondently. "What do you mean, Mark, the answer lies in the soil?"

"Well, as you may be aware, various Canaanite sites have been excavated by archaeologists in the Israel of today. You may also be aware that the Canaanites spoke a Semitic language closely related to Hebrew and this fact is mentioned not only in the Bible but also in Mesopotamian and Ancient Egyptian texts."

"So what you are really saying, Mark, is that the Israelis may well have a strong claim to ancestral lands?"

"Yes, and the claim is probably stronger when you realise that Canaan approximates today as Israel, the West Bank and Gaza, plus the adjoining coastal lands and parts of the Lebanon and Syria. Moreover, Ibby, when you study the Jewish version of the Bible, in fact the Hebrew Bible or Tanakh, this includes books common to both my own Christian and Jewish biblical canons. These officially accepted collectionsof religious writings are further reinforced in the Jewish Torah. This book has a very loose similarity with your Qur'an and the entries in their Torah are considered by most Jews to be God's direct words; Jewish religious law is therefore derived from the Torah. The Torah tells us how God commanded Abraham to leave his family and home in the city of Ur, to eventually settle in Canaan."

"So what was the situation in Biblical times, Mark?"

"The Israelites, of whom you will have heard, were the dominant cultural and ethnic group living in Canaan. This area was composed of the Kingdom of Israel, obliterated by the Assyrians, and Judah which was conquered by Babylon. The Persians as you know then conquered Babylon and allowed the deportation of the former Israelites back to their homeland. Mainstream Judaism really began when these deportees returned and began to rebuild their Temple. What is more significant, Ibby, is that all modern Jews claim to be descendants of these original tribes, hence the Twelve Tribes of Israel. Scholars of biblical genealogy continue to delve into the origins of the Tribes, of course."

"Their true origins I guess become more important as they press their territorial claims, Mark?"

"Why yes, and it is even more important today to learn this, as modern historians all know perfectly well that for a number of complex reasons by Roman times very few Jews actually lived in their Promised Land."

"And, today, Mark?"

"Well, Ibby, we saw the rise of Zionism that changed the situation in Palestine irrevocably. Following those violent attacks in the late 1800s on Jewish communities in Russia, the displaced then called themselves the 'Lovers of Zion' and sought a return to their homeland that God had given them; that homeland was, of course, Palestine. The Jews created a global sense of urgency, they established their World Zionist Organisation and it wasn't long before mass migration back to Jerusalem began. You mentioned Ben Gurion, Ibby, well it was he who master-minded the Zionist campaign and generated the Zionist Provisional State Council which finally declared, that which all Jews had long dreamed of, a State of Israel."

"Aye, Mark. I think we can all now understand the Israeli position more clearly, but Palestinians can also prove their ancient historical claims and that they were there long before recent Jewish migration happened. The Palestinians feel they have more right to the holy places for the fact they were there throughout history. Also lands traditionally have been won or lost in the Middle East by war and not by historical claims to anciently held tribal lands?"

"True, Ibby and on this point I will never forget the words of that Likud hard-liner, Benjamin Netanyahu who said: 'Jewish sovereignty and Jewish power are the only deterrents and only guarantees against the slaughter of the Jews,' and this view remains widespread in Israel to this day."

Milford Sound in the south-west corner of New Zealand seemed a most unrealistic place on the globe for the aspirations of Mark and Ibrahim to unfold. However, the clarity and absolute tranquillity of this exceptionally scenic and remote corner of New Zealand, little seen or even known by most in the world, was not on this day but was normally one of the wettest places on earth and certainly, the wettest in New Zealand! The Sound, or more accurately it should be classified as a fjord, had a mean annual rainfall of 6813 mm on 182 days a year. This was a high level even for the West Coast of New Zealand which boasted the best of the rain forests. Rainfall at the Sound could reach 250 mm during a span of 24 hours. Recognising this, Ibrahim and his family and Mark took to the highway in their 4WD vehicles to make one of the finest overland trips to Milford. It was a cloudless day, cool but with brilliant sunshine, almost unknown locally to ever occur for so long an unbroken period.

"Well, Ibby, we are fortunate with the weather but I am still concerned about the road conditions with all this snow and ice about," motioned Mark.

"We will look at the situation, Mark, again, after we get to Te Anau and that large lake you mentioned."

"Sure, we have tyre chains but if we have to use them that will slow us down to less than 20 kmph and we will not be able to get back to Queenstown until well after nightfall when the ice on the roads will be worse than ever ………"

"Let's try anyway," reaffirmed Ibrahim cautiously. They were pouring over the road maps outside their Queenstown hotel with the family already and waiting in the vehicles. "We have no time to waste!"

Certainly it was going to be a long drive but no sooner were they off then all Mark's fears of poor road conditions evaporated. The roads were dry and ice-free. Excellent time was made to Te Anau whereupon it was resolved to proceed apace. Stopping to wander around the town of Te Anau and dream around the lake was a thought overshadowed by the imminent challenge to get to Milford Sound. It was the only deep fjord accessible by road and all the indicators were that the road was not only open, a rare event in itself, but was beckoning them and their adventurous spirit to respond. With this oneness to press on, the challenge reminded Mark of a lovely old Scottish rhyme:

> *'Oh, piper, let us be up and gone!*
> *We'll follow you quick if you pipe us on,*
> *For all of us want to be there.'*

Kilometre after kilometre slipped by; the land of rugged mountains, steep gorges and narrow passes coupled with enchanting vast beech forests, water-falls frozen in time with luxuriously deep green mosses, ferns and grasses clinging to rock faces, all enshrined in icicles, formed a visual tapestry second to none. It was a landscape forged by the rapid retreat of the great glaciers and was a human journey and unique experience, into a wilderness of astounding geological diversity on a breathtaking scale. Rank upon rank of snow-tipped peaks passed and finally the vehicles were brought to an unexpected and abrupt halt outside the entrance to what clearly was a tunnel. With signs which said: 'switch headlights on', it was none other than the Homer Tunnel.

The Homer Tunnel, some 1.2 kms in length and 945 m above sea level, pierced the Main Divide of the Southern Alps at the head of the Hollyford Valley, a relatively short distance from the Milford Sound itself. It was in 1889 when a W.H.Homer who discovered the saddle, later to bear his name, suggested a tunnel through the ridge below the saddle. Many years elapsed and finally excavation began at the close of the years of the Great Depression in 1935. It took five years to dig that tunnel, almost all by hand with primitive equipment and the light 'at the end of the tunnel' began to shine in 1940. Work was suspended during the World Wars and in 1945 a very large avalanche severely damaged the eastern portal almost calling for closure. However, work resumed after World War II was over and the tunnel, to everyone's delight, was finally completed and opened in 1953, the year of the Coronation of Her Majesty Queen Elizabeth II.

Slowly, very slowly, Mark and Ibrahim inched their vehicles through the narrow and dimly lit tunnel, the floor of which, water-logged in part, was undulating and had the effect of a drive along the spine of a slippery serpent! Once through, with the towering peaks of the Darren Mountains at the rear, the road turned and descended past the Milford Lodge, one of very few places of accommodation, to the jetty landing. There it was, Mitre Peak, 1,692m, which stood in all its glory as the sentinel of the Sound. Snow clad, and silent, it was simply a stunning sight and no wonder was regarded the iconic mountain of this remote location. It was named by one of the crew on board the earliest visits of the survey ship, HMS *Acheron,* and no doubt today what was observed was identical to that seen years ago.

In the foreground the deep icy blue to green water was absolutely still; this was the head of the inlet which, if followed, would lead to the open turbulence of the Tasman Sea. Mark momentarily adjusted his sun glasses and softly spoke to Ibrahim: "Would you believe, Ibby, that just below the surface of these waters is black coral?"

"Black coral?" exclaimed a startled Ibrahim.

"Aye, black coral. You know the stuff we used to dream about when we dived in your tropical waters." Mark and Ibrahim had both dived extensively and knew only too well how rare this endangered tree-like coral was; it was related they knew to the sea anemone and though its living tissue was brightly coloured it was the distinctive black to dark brown skeleton which gave it its name. "In Hawaii," Mark continued joyously, "it is the official State gem but here we are just blessed to have this treasure with us and so near to the surface too; in summer and good light it can be seen from a glass bottom boat."

"Now, Mark, have you any more surprises for me?" enquired a curious Ibrahim.

"Possibly just one more," Mark paused, "Milford Sound is at the southern end of one of our three World Heritage sites."

"You make me laugh, Mark. Only THREE sites! The whole of the Middle East is a World Heritage Site; The Pyramids, Valley of the Kings, Petra, the Roman cities, Jordon, Lebanon, Syria; the list is endless!"

"I can hear your love of Shakespeare coming to the fore, Ibby: *Friends, Romans, countrymen, lend me your ears......*"

"You jest, Mark, but the historical value of the Middle East is second to none!"

"Aye, I appreciate that, Ibby, and even now new archaeological findings keep appearing thousands of years later. Seriously, Ibby, what you have in the Middle East goes back well before any list of World Heritage Sites; yours is the home to the origins of The Seven Wonders of the World."

"Of course, Mark. The Pyramids of Egypt; the Hanging Gardens of Babylon; the Pharos of Alexandria; and do you remember with your classical education the remainder, Mark?"

"I think so, Ibby: the Tomb of Mausolus; the Temple of Diana at Ephesus; the Statue of Jupiter, by Phidias and, yes, the Colossus of Rhodes. Then the list of the seven wonders changed as did our scholars and generations."

"I think," added Ibby with a smile, "they soon included the Great Wall of China and the Leaning Tower of Pisa."

"Ah, that reminds me. Big Ben once wrote a love letter to Pisa. It read: *I have the time, if you have the inclination!*"

"And did Pisa reply?"

"Ben," Pisa had replied: *"I have always been bent on you!"*

Mark proudly recounted that four National Parks of southern New Zealand collectively formed one World Heritage site known by the Maori name of *Te Wahipounamu*. The Parks included Westland, Mt Aspiring, Mt Cook and Fiordland. The good fortune of the isolation of the south-west corner, covering some 10 percent of the country, meant that this Heritage site had been little changed by human beings and their influences since the beginning of time. Above all, too, the area possessed some of the world's finest examples of Gondwanaland, the southern hemisphere, where flora and fauna had remained in its natural habitat.

"We will be seeing Mt Cook National Park soon, Ibby. Cook is at the northern end of this Heritage site. We do have three World Heritage sites at present with possibly more to come. The second Heritage site is in the North Island, the Tongariro National Park, and the third site we sadly cannot access as it constitutes five Sub-Antarctic island groups off the south coast of New Zealand. You may have heard of the islands: the Snares, Bounty, Antipodes, Auckland and Campbell islands. They are sanctuaries for the large number and diversity of pelagic seabirds and penguins that nest there."

"You said, Mark, that you may have some more sites?"

"Well we have just recently hosted the 31st Session of the World Heritage Committee in Christchurch, the second time the meeting has been held in Australasia in the past 20 years and the first for New Zealand since adoption of the Convention in 1972 in the UN. Over a thousand delegates and observers attended and we did submit a string of potential new sites for the Committee to consider. So we are more than optimistic!"

The family returned to Queenstown via Lake Te Anau on the same road as they entered; there was no other way at present. For those who had little time this quadrant of remote New Zealand of course could be explored by air and rather than miss it, in fine weather, the air option with a landing on Milford's very small airstrip remained a practical but costly solution. However, the visionaries of the future were already working on plans to either put in a monorail or a system of new tunnels, or both, to connect Queenstown more directly to Milford. The monorail concept had the greatest support and the local authority was now charged with examining the proposal in detail. One could only hope in this modern world of technology that such an innovation would not take the years that pioneers suffered in creating the Homer Tunnel and that environmentalists would not block or delay the progress of mankind in the quest to bring more of the people closer to their heritage. With the monorail very much a dream for Ibrahim he pressed on back to Queenstown.

With a backdrop of a western shore of lush virgin forest and the surrounding hill country of the Mount Luxmore and Murchison mountains, when Lake Te Anau had come once again into sight, Ibrahim pulled the vehicles alongside a small, rickety wooden jetty. The serene deep waters of the Lake were flat in the breathless conditions. Just as the light of the long day was disappearing, the family enjoyed once more one of those rare and special moments in touch with nature as it always had been. The absolute peace that prevailed was a perfect ending to that one day in a million at Milford.

So it may have been a peaceful day but after dinner that night, an almost exhausted Mark was approached by Ibrahim whose mind had been racing on the question of Arab–Israeli relations.

"Mark, do you know the one most disturbing reality we have to continually put up with our Israeli neighbours is their open confrontational policy. Perhaps it is this aspect of their politics I detest most. I will never forget when Ariel Sharon visited our Al Aqsa Mosque in September 2000."

"In East Jerusalem?"

"Yes."

"The world witnessed the aftermath on television, Ibby. I recall the incident as if it happened today. I can see that innocent Arab 12-year-old boy being shot several times by Israeli soldiers as chaos and mayhem erupted in the wake of the visit. It is no wonder that the Second, or perhaps more correctly called, the Palestinian Al Aqsa Intifada rose so sharply afterwards."

"So what hope do you hold for the resumption of the Road Map, Mark?"

"Ibby, every time I hear the words, Road Map, I automatically think of an old schoolboy jingle:

'The rule of the road is paradox quite,
In riding or driving along;
If you go to the left you are sure to go right,
If you go to the right you go wrong!'

"But seriously, Ibby, if there ever was a Rule of the Road, then the Quartet of the UN, USA, Europe, and Russia that set this dialogue initially in motion in 2002 have failed to persevere! The tension remains as high as ever in real life."

"Well Mark, both the Israeli Prime Minister Ehud Olmert and Palestinian President Mahmoud Abbas have also again more recently failed to bridge the gap. I see Abbas is now striving for a Middle East Conference with the revised objective of a framework agreement for peace with Israel, with a new time-line for implementation."

4

Mount Cook – Women and Marriage

"If there is any one single issue," pleaded Rabab, "that is so widely misunderstood and misrepresented in the West, it is our position on women in Islam." Rabab continued, "There has been an overwhelming onslaught of press misinformation and gross overstatement, exaggeration in fact, about us in the film and television industry. I was never so appalled as when I caught an episode of a daytime TV programme when I was in London, and learned about the Bahraini 'princess' who wanted to marry an American Marine. If that wasn't bad enough I later happened to see another family show which told us of women under Taliban rule in Afghanistan and again, an entire feature film which showed how an American woman was violated by a husband who went mad on his return to Iran."

"Viewers in the West must think we are all trapped in some kind of time capsule sealed in the Dark Ages!" added Farah excitedly.

"Fortunately, Rabab, television also ensures that we *don't* live in the Dark Ages!" noted Mark with growing concern for the feelings of his youthful lady passengers and, attempting to change the subject, he proffered warily, "You will surely have seen the *Discovery Channel?*"

Mark was driving and had Ibrahim's daughters, Rabab and Farah, as his rear-seat companions. Khamis remained as 'navigator' in the front. Noticeably, Khamis was unusually quiet and listened perhaps for the first time about how his sisters really felt about the apparent subjugation of their gender in Islamic society. He really hadn't seriously given any thought to this topic nor had he ever perhaps considered their inner feelings. His school work and sport had always preoccupied his time. Zamzam was in the other car with his mother and father but Khamis knew that Rabab and Farah were much brighter than he was academically. So he was following the debate now very carefully. At home with his sisters always around he also wasn't in any frame of mind to ever rush into marriage either! In fact this was the last thing presently on his mind.

Upon reflection and with deeper thought, Mark decided to encourage his lady passengers to freely talk about their concerns about womanhood and their rights.

"You may be amazed" he began, "that the simple practice of giving a wedding ring in marriage is common throughout many religions of the world. Yet, the ring predates Roman times. There is nothing theological or in our Christian faith that directs the use of a ring, yet it is a custom that we are all familiar with and adopt."

"What you are saying," volunteered Khamis who suddenly now took an interest, "is that we have requirements of faith and also customs?"

"Yes, and we should draw distinct lines between these two as confusion is generated through ignorance."

"So if we look at subjects more closely we will be able to sort the wheat from the chaff. I for one," initiated an enlivened Khamis, "know that circumcision is not considered a religious sacrament in Islam but is performed as a more practical function related to good health and hygiene."

"Yes; for men," added Mark promptly. "Again look back: this practice pre-dates recorded human history with pictures in Stone Age cave drawings and ancient Egyptian tombs. Indeed it is only a commandment in Judaism, Khamis," Mark paused, "expected in Islam, yes of course, and customary in some Oriental and Orthodox churches. More importantly," Mark turned to the girls who were spellbound by the topic, "female circumcision is neither required by Islam nor encouraged."

"I thought circumcision was just a male thing," added Khamis bemusedly.

"No! It is not a problem for you, Khamis, but for poorly educated womenfolk it is and in many African communities the practice is still widespread," sparked Farah sharply.

This broad-minded approach to a 'sensitive' subject encouraged an enthusiastic development in the discussion. After all these three youngsters, boy and two girls alike, were exceptionally well educated, so Mark pressed on, changing the direction of the debate: "So, ladies, just what are some of the positive aspects for which Islam genuinely gives support?"

Silence for a moment saw the girls glance at each other in thought then almost a torrent of ideas flooded the cabin.

"For a start," began Rabab, "we cannot be denied the right to an equal education; we cannot be forced into marriage; and yes, we can vote and stand for civil office and many women hold high appointments."

Khamis proudly advised Mark, "Women have held Cabinet portfolios such as Higher Education; Tourism; Crafts; Economics, Health and other senior Offices. We continue to see this trend not only in the Gulf States but across the broader spectrum of the Islamic World as in Pakistan and Bangladesh."

"Thank you, Khamis, I did not know that but I have known for many years just how advanced women are within the Islamic world. And ladies," Mark again turned to the girls, "what happens in marriage?"

"Well, a woman's property cannot be seized by her husband; a man cannot ruin a woman's reputation; and we can initiate a divorce if we want to."

"And, about divorce?"

"Women can file legal suits in courts; we can provide sole testimony; we do also get automatic custody of our young children; and we get what you call alimony, the money to maintain ourselves."

At this point Khamis was beginning to realise just how serious a potential marriage pact would be if he should decide one day to follow that perhaps inevitable route. These girls certainly knew what their rights were and they knew too that if they were ever abused by a husband they could immediately seek legal redress. Islam did not encourage the oppression of women and indeed, to the contrary, Islam actively sought to promote the protection of women's rights.

"So where do having rights on one hand," Mark observed patiently, "and having customs on another, actually cause this cultural collision with the West?"

"Well, like the wedding ring, our women through lack of education and genuine illiteracy in the past have had to rely on the fanaticism or otherwise of the clerics and their husbands in telling them what is right or wrong, so customs have emerged which have falsely been believed to be Islamic. This we have most recently seen with the severity of the Taliban in Afghanistan whose extreme implementation of apparent rules bears little to no relation with the real teachings of Islam. As you have mentioned before, Mark, the Taliban have never been seen by mainstream Islam to be politically legitimate." Rabab spoke with increasing conviction.

"Most of the customs which are seen in the West to be controversial normally stem from these tribal influences, not religious edicts. Tribalism remains strong and only with education will we see some of the time-ancient practices actually stop. In many parts of Islamic Africa what is going on will take us a century or more to halt, including female circumcision!"

This was a passionate plea. The car rolled on for several kilometres before discussion resumed; it was all a beneficial learning experience.

"Did you ever wear a hat to school?" enquired a curious Khamis.

"Why of course!" said Mark wonderingly.

"Well, I don't think many kids do that these days."

"Yes and no, Khamis. Lads who are privileged to have a really good and comprehensive education at one of our private colleges certainly will wear a hat, summer and winter."

"But at the State schools here in New Zealand?"

"Rarely, I admit, do the boys or girls wear hats but in some schools the tradition remains."

"So it would be very unusual and exceptionally obvious for one of our girls to wear her Islamic scarf over her hair in one of your schools?" The questioning came from Khamis to the surprise of Rabab and Farah who remained silent at the back of the car.

"No," intoned Mark thoughtfully, "New Zealand is a multi-cultural nation and we have young Sikhs with turbans appearing in a number of our schools, particularly around Auckland, so if some Arabian girls were enrolled their dress codes would be explained to classmates. Why do you ask, Khamis?"

"Well, when we were in France on an exchange student arrangement recently, a complete embargo was placed on our people wearing religiously associated clothing. There was a lot of hostility towards us and ill-feeling on both sides."

"Yes, I understand that, Khamis. The French sadly have unsubstantiated fears of an erosion of their traditional customs; their language for one has been overshadowed by the fixation in the minds of modern youth, globally, that they need to learn English, not French."

"We call the 'scarf', Mark, the *hijab* or *Khimar* and this is one item we are required to wear publicly, plus clothes which are loose fitting so as to detract from an outward appearance of glamour. Another profound misunderstanding in the West, Mark, is that all women are required by Islam to wear a veil over the face, the *niqab*, and wearing that all too often described billowing full length dress, the *burqa*, with socks and gloves. These are simply not a requirement of Islam. Once again, Mark, the women who do wear these more restrictive and restrained forms of dress do so largely because of years of tribal custom and the unqualified insistence of their less advantaged or educated men-folk."

"Personally, Rabab, I do not find the wearing of the *hijab* in any way offensive. My mother, and indeed Her Majesty the Queen of England, admittedly for different reasons, always wore either a scarf over their hair or a hat. As Defender of the Faith and Head of the Church of England, furthermore, the Queen would never be seen without a hat in the execution of her public duties. In fact her milliner quite often attaches a veil to her hats. Again for a different reason, at funerals almost all women would wear a black hat of sorts with a veil through which the face could not be seen. Also, Her Majesty always attends church services with full length sleeves and gloves and a long dress. The fact that many of her subjects choose to ignore the correct etiquette of dress merely demonstrates a lack of breeding! You will never see the aristocracy or ladies of the Diplomatic Corps in Britain or overseas, or ladies in society, improperly or incorrectly dressed!"

"Mark, you may not be aware, that we do *not* hide our womenfolk away in their homes. This is an old custom called *purdah* and certainly has no foundation in our true Islamic faith. Some people now in very few countries continue with this custom and they distort world opinion and attitudes towards our faith. They do us no favour by persisting with these outmoded and culturally archaic customs," Farah clearly was incensed by the attitudes of so many followers of Islam.

"Farah, you are exceptionally fortunate to have parents who are both moderate in their Islamic views and exceptionally well educated; just think if you were locked up by the Taliban virtually never to see the light of day?"

"I hate to think of it, Mark," said a relieved Farah. As the day had progressed a much happier and more contented set of passengers had relaxed into their mode of travel.

"One point that does concern me," rejoined Farah enthusiastically, "is the misconception that the Arab can have many wives."

"Ah yes, Farah," Mark began, "it is a common misunderstanding, I agree."

"What people don't understand," Farah continued plausibly, "is that we women are not in favour of polygamy. In fact the conditions to permit more than one wife, set within Islam, are extremely tight indeed."

"Ninety-nine percent," Rabab rejoined also enthusiastically, "of marriages in our Muslim world are with a single woman. This is because the Qur'an rules that a man must treat us fairly in all things. Each wife must be treated equally both in time and money and no favouritism is allowed. If our husbands do choose to have another wife then in many ways it works in our favour as the added commitment ties the man to each wife so much so that he cannot relinquish his responsibilities. But we still prefer a 'one wife' relationship, although up to four wives are permitted."

Khamis offered an opinion cautiously, "I believe it all started because of war when if there was a shortage of men, only a limited number of women would find husbands. Isn't that right, Mark?"

"Well, Khamis, firstly, yes, and secondly, you may also be surprised to learn that both in Judaism and Christianity men were allowed to have multiple wives but that practice disappeared in the Middle Ages. Apart from war, too, medical knowledge was scarce in the old days and many women would have died during child birth. The mortality rate of the children was also high until quite recent times. So in many ways it was a survival of the species concept. Today, with good medical services a lot of the old problems and reasons for additional wives have disappeared. Also the family economics would preclude most men from even thinking of a second wife!"

"Some of us also want to pursue careers, Mark," motioned Rabab studiously.

"Yes, times have changed and thinking must also change. I believe the misconception in the West stems both from ignorance and a misguided form of jealousy, particularly among our lower socio-economic group of individuals who do not, in many instances, place much value in the concept and institution of marriage. Over the last 50 years we have also seen a marked increase in Western promiscuity fuelled by an over dramatised film industry and a more profligate Hollywood that has turned the image of women into purely sex objects! So we have a lot of rethinking to do in the West with a greater emphasis and priority to be placed on human and moral values."

Abel Tasman (1603–1659), Dutch seafarer, explorer and merchant, was the first European in December 1642 to sight New Zealand. He named it Staten Landt believing it was connected to an island, Staten Land in Argentina, at the tip of South America. Although he engaged in battles with the Maoris he did not step foot on New Zealand. Historians more recently, however, have came to believe that some of his sailors may have actually landed. It was after this great seafarer that many locations in Australasia had been named, principally Tasmania and the Tasman Sea. In New Zealand the second highest peak, Mount Tasman, 3497m and its adjacent glacier, the Tasman Glacier, all 27 kilometres of it, carry his name.

It was to Captain James Cook of the Royal Navy (1728–1779), an English explorer, navigator and cartographer, that the highest esteem was accorded, however, as he was the first to circumnavigate New Zealand and the first to establish permanent links with Britain. The highest peak in Australasia, Mount Cook, 3754m, proudly recalls his name albeit the Maoris have also added their claim and name to this peak as *Aoraki*.

Ibrahim, his family and Mark were heading straight for Mount Cook on this day and would remain there for awhile at the Hermitage, Mount Cook Village. Weather conditions continued to be supreme as the broad anti-cyclone sat comfortably over the whole of the South Island. Clear blue skies, sunshine and wind-free chilly days were the norm with severe, sub-zero, overnight temperatures as a consequence. Lake Pukaki, the glacially-fed lake at the lower end of the Tasman Glacier, would normally in summer months reflect its glacial input with a vivid turquoise hue but today, as the family approached the Hermitage, the Lake cast colours of a distinctly steel-cold veneer of greys and black pierced only on its banks by trees, fences and fields frozen with a pure white hoar frost that refused to melt. It was extremely cold.

Undeterred by the cold, after booking in at the hotel, Ibrahim took the family for an exploratory walk around the small village, all of which was snugly fit into a glove of design compatible with the environment. Mount Cook Village, with its tiny community of just a few houses, was a far cry from, and a complete opposite to, the commercial thrust and overtones of Queenstown. Mount Cook National Park was not only the northern end of the World Heritage site, of which Milford Sound was also a part, but it was the focal point of an alpine-rich mountaineering centre whose enthusiasts were eco-conscious and protective of the country-side in the extreme. Mark was one of them, a former very active moun-taineer, who had spent many months climbing in this region.

Over the topographical relief model of the Park, in the Visitors' Centre, Mark described how he and others had climbed Mount Cook some 30 years earlier in his much younger adult years. He was then a very active member of a mountain search and rescue team. Cook was a climb in severity, comparable in length and difficulty to ascents of the Arguille Verte in Chamonix, France and Mount Huntington in Alaska. He pointed out the finer details of the Zurbriggen Ridge, named after a Swiss guide who pioneered many of the climbing routes in the early 1900s, and the Linda Glacier route which he had taken to the summit. For Mark, this visit to Mount Cook also brought back vivid memories of his pioneering flight over the peak of Cook in his hot air balloon, an adventure captured on film by New Zealand Television for posterity.

No visit to the Park, enthused Mark, would be complete without a flight over the whole of it and a landing by ski-plane on the upper snow field of the Tasman Glacier was a 'must'. To this end, Ibrahim and his family ventured forth to meet this challenge. It was a Harry Wigley, a New Zealander, who saw the need for a retractable ski which would allow aeroplanes to take off from an airfield and land on snow. On 22nd September 1955 he piloted his Auster aircraft and made the first such landing, using his skis, on the upper Tasman Glacier. Today, Mount Cook Ski Planes operated both Cessna 185 aircraft and Pilatus Turbo Porter PC6 Swiss aircraft, both of which had a high wing configuration and slow flying speed that allowed first-class viewing of the great pan-theon of peaks. On touch down on the snow, with the engine turned off, only the distant rumble of the occasional avalanche would have disturbed the natural quiet of the mountains. This landing on snow in the high alpine air of New Zealand, for an Arabian family, was a major milestone in their inventory of life experiences.

5

Christchurch – Islam in Daily Life

─────────

"Well Ibrahim, we have left the snow and ice now a long way behind us. Gone are the picture postcard winter scenes of our highest alpine region."

"Yes, Mark. It was good, however, to be in touch with nature and know that part of the world has not changed in centuries. It gives one a stronger sense of self-belief when we see nature frozen in solitude."

"Well I admire the courage of your family to brace themselves against the elements of our winter in the South Island. Most New Zealanders shun this part of the country and head north but as you have seen, no doubt, on television our so-called 'winterless north', much further north than Auckland, has had heavy rain and thunderstorms over the last two weeks which has, of course, generated extensive flooding with many roads closed. It is just as well you opted to start your journey in Queenstown."

"We have to take what comes, Mark!" said a deeply pleased Ibrahim. "Now we only have one night in Christchurch before we do in fact start heading north; is that right?"

"Yes."

"I want the family to see the Antarctic Centre near the airport, Mark, and do some more shopping. Queenstown really was just a tourist centre and catered largely for the skiing fraternity. I understand your brother was able to track down a pair of shoes for Khamis?"

"Yes, that task you would have thought plain sailing but then when one shoe outlet after another unsympathetically says that they have no such size in stock, one wonders just how lads like Khamis can actually get a pair of shoes."

"Well, I don't know what Mona has been feeding him on recently but he has shot up in height so swiftly that his feet are now big enough to support the weight of a Sumo wrestler!"

"Or an Olympic basketball player?" suggested Mark with a smile. "Well my brother," Mark explained, "knows Christchurch well. He lives just north of central Christchurch by the way and he has tracked down a shop in Colombo Street, close to your hotel and tells me the owner has three pairs of shoes of the size 50 or US 12.5, UK 11, FR50 or for the real Sumo, a Japanese 300 is available!"

"We will get down tonight."

"Don't leave it too late, Ibby," cautioned Mark, "Christchurch shops in winter start closing at 5 o'clock!"

"Goodness, that early?"

"Well central city shops do stop open to perhaps 6.30 in the evening but with winter you never can tell. In fact, Ibby, I once heard an American describe the winter scene of Christchurch as a cemetery with stop and go lights!"

That evening, Khamis was in luck. Two pairs of his very size of shoe were suitable. Thankfully, at last, he was able to jettison the pair of trainers he had, the sole on one of which had parted company.

The American in fact was not too far from the truth as most of the people of Christchurch do quickly disappear into the warmth of their homes and the streets of the city do become bleak and bare of human kind as the nights advance. Although it was the regional centre of the farming community of Canterbury and New Zealand's second largest city, after Auckland, it was also a very conservative community which did not depend on a thriving night life to sustain its interests. Christchurch was just that bit different; indeed it was not only regarded as the English garden city but it was the most English of cities in New Zealand. Today too, Christchurch was heavily populated with students as here were two State universities and a myriad collection of English language schools and technical colleges. The faces seen about the pavements were those of young Chinese, Japanese and Thai men and women on budget incomes who strived to advance their personal skills. They had come to the right place; after all, the city was designed by the early Canterbury Pilgrims to be a city around a cathedral and college modelled on Christ Church college of Oxford, England. This outpost of English traditionalism was settled and founded in 1848. The Maoris told us, however, in song that they had settled here first, from the Pacific Islands centuries earlier. Archaeological evidence found near the city in 1876 had indeed confirmed that moa-hunting tribes did exist about 1250. The moa was a giant flightless bird some 3.6 m in height and 250 kg in weight. Several remains of these ostrich-like creatures had been found and were preserved in our museums. It apparently was hunted and driven into extinction by an also extinct bird, the Haast Eagle, the world's largest eagle. Clearly Christchurch was a vastly different place then!

"Mark, we are proud of our Islamic heritage," pressed a concerned Khamis who was once again in the navigator's seat as the vehicles steadily moved onward and northward. Today the family was leaving Christchurch behind. They had seen the Antarctic Centre but being the last week of the New Zealand school holidays it was overrun, naturally, by the school children for which it was principally designed. Mark was actually disappointed with the Centre as in its efforts to provide for a pro-active very youthful audience, much of the integrity of the polar efforts by the pioneers had been overshadowed by modern interactive gimmickry.

"So why is your Mohammed the Prophet so important to you, Khamis?" enquired Mark, who was now well accustomed to listening to the various Qur'anic CDs as they were periodically fed to the music centre on the dash board.

"He is our very special hero, Mark."

"Why, because he established Islam?"

"Oh much more than that, Mark."

"I am listening, Khamis," smiled Mark curiously as the volume on the CD was reduced.

"Well, you asked why he is so important to us and my answer is quite simple really. Our Prophet Mohammed gave us our classical Arabic of the Qur'an and with it a new literary language. With the Qur'an we were all able to receive the word of Allah as it was revealed to Mohammed by the Archangel Gabriel."

"Ah, now that is an interesting viewpoint, Khamis. You know, some people in the West think you pray to Mohammed?"

"No we don't!" exclaimed Khamis utterly surprised, "we pray to Allah!"

"So once again Khamis we see a misconception in the West?"

"Yes, Allah is our one and only god and Mohammed the Prophet is his messenger."

"Coming back to my point then," pursued Mark, "why is Mohammed so important in your daily lives apart from his historical contribution?"

Khamis gave some deep thought again to the topic. Here was a man challenging him to identify the very core of his Islamic identity and philosophy. He knew if his father was present, he would want him to answer Mark truthfully and as he turned his head towards the rear seats, his sisters both visually spurred him on; their looks alone convinced him that he was required now to defend his faith.

"Well," he began, "we pray to Allah regularly so that we can keep in touch with our faith. This gives us our strength to face the day and the night and combat the difficulties we may encounter. Our prayers give us a peace of mind and help us reduce the stresses and strains of life."

"Character building and personal discipline, perhaps?" prompted Mark.

"Yes. Above all our Prophet Mohammed is our teacher who gives us the guidance to live our lives. He is the mentor whose experience of life in turn we can follow. Without his teachings, drawn from the wisdom embodied in the Qur'an, our lives would be almost meaningless. He has forged, especially for us, the relationship between Allah and ourselves, indeed between Allah and the whole of mankind. His guidance also defines for us the pathway we must walk, and the choices we must make, between heaven and hell."

Mark reflected upon these comments and glancing at Khamis, he saw in that lad's face the sincerity of someone much more advanced than his years. He wondered to himself that if he had asked a similar question of a lad of equal age from his Anglican church whether he would have been so wisely informed. For Khamis and all those like him, the Prophet Mohammed was no longer the young man born in a sixth-century Arabia who walked among the flocks, the caravans and the markets of Mecca but was a living, personal counsellor in his daily presence. The importance of the Prophet Mohammed was paramount as it was through him that not only the beauty of the Qur'an was exposed to mankind but also the pattern and framework was outlined for the very preservation of civilisation itself.

"Thank you, Khamis. Clarifying the doctrines of Islam, indeed of any religion, is a monumental task but with your daily prayers the world can see, without question, your declaration of faith of which you must be proud."

"I am," interjected a jubilant Khamis, "and Allah is forgiving and bountiful in his rewards," thien even more jubilantly, Khamis pronounced: "our Islamic era, the Hegira, began when our Prophet Mohammed and Abu Bakr escaped from Mecca to the oasis of Yathrib, which we now call Medina, on the 15th June in your year AD 622. Our world then changed!"

"Abu Bakr?"

"Mark, Abu Bakr was Mohammed's first important non-family convert."

"Ah, thank you, Khamis, and when was the first pilgrimage to Mecca?"

"During a truce; many battles occurred in those early years. It was year seven of the new era. That would make that great and historic event in your year AD 629. So you can see, Mark, we have a wonderful history of devotion and leadership which now has spread throughout the world."

Khamis reflected the very image of his father. It was Ibrahim's inner strength that empowered him to not only bring his whole family to New Zealand to extend the boundaries of their knowledge but also to permit them to see for themselves the human race in a wider context and perspective. After all, they were now a Muslim family in a predominantly Christian country and albeit a small community of Muslims did reside in New Zealand, they were exploring new ground with new objectives and different ideals. They truly were foreign travellers in a foreign land. Ibrahim was like a modern Marco Polo! Recognising this cultural gap, it was clear that the strength of Ibrahim's union with his family rested in something much stronger than the material things of life. Indeed their adherence to the word and teachings of the Prophet Mohammed was that inner strength; possessing this alone would allow them to rise above all worldly things and reach those levels of human understanding that only came to those whose vision and commitment to Islam was intact. Prophet Mohammed clearly was of overwhelming importance to Muslims in their everyday life and this was visibly demonstrated in their prayers and acts to their fellow man.

Kaikoura, 180 kms north of Christchurch, was the family's first stop. 'Kaikoura' was Maori and meant: kai = eat, and koura = crayfish. Not surprisingly, therefore, everyone wanted to eat some crayfish for lunch and as the peninsula, upon which Kaikoura had developed, actually projected into the nearby depths of the Hikurangi Trench there was an abundance of marine life along this spectacular coastline. Sperm whales offshore were a noted tourist attraction plus, along the rocks, the Southern Fur seal had made a home for itself with dolphins also a common sight. High in the air too, at times, the great mariners' albatross would also soar. It was a place where the snow-capped Seaward Kaikoura Mountains almost touched the sea.

It was perhaps no surprise that Mark pulled up outside "The Lobster Inn", visible by its large imitation fibreglass, red crayfish on the roof. What was a surprise, however, was that after they entered it was immediately apparent that the locals were avidly following and gambling on a horse-race meeting screened on the multiple television monitors that adorned the walls. The only interruption of the race meeting was flashes of the All Blacks, the nation's rugby football players. Coupled with this visual indulgence, a game of pool was in progress in one room while the country locals were very happily sinking large volumes of beer. For this pub's clientele of 'regulars' it really was a wake-up call with a difference when Ibrahim and his family entered the room. However, tolerance of others' beliefs was one of New Zealand's greatest attributes and they showed no concern; after all, their ritual of 'rugby, racing and beer' was their tradition steeped in custom from time immemorial! This display of decadence in a conservative Islamic society would of course not exist but Ibrahim's family was not deterred; a sign, also on one wall, boasted of the prowess of this pub in producing the finest meals in town! Indeed, as the family discovered, the Chef must have abandoned all hope of watching the rugby or the racing and produced some of the finest meals experienced on the journey to-date.

The final leg of the day's journey took them over roads from which they saw seemingly endless rows upon rows of grapes under cultivation. They had entered one of the largest wine-producing regions in Australasia – Marlborough. They were to stop-over in Blenheim, a country town, at the very heart of this wine and gourmet food industry where such names as Chardonnay and Sauvignon Blanc were on the tips of all the tongues. As the day drew to a close, Mark thought to himself just how lucky New Zealand was, not to have been blessed with the wrath of the Taliban. If they were mad enough to have destroyed the 2000-year-old ancient Buddha statues in the Bamiyan Valley, what destruction would they have brought upon the vineyards of New Zealand? It didn't bear thinking about but he had solace that night in the knowledge that Ibrahim, and mainstream Islamic society, saw the Taliban merely as misguided vandals bereft of normal tolerant Islamic values.

6

Marlborough – Arab and Western Alliances

"Most people in the West conveniently forget," motioned Ibrahim, "that almost all the Islamic states supported the overthrow of the tyrant Saddam Hussein. Jordon noticeably declined but we cannot blame them as they probably were just too close to Saddam for comfort. We have consistently demonstrated that if we in Arabia make an agreement we stick to it; our word is as good the handshake of an Englishman!"

"You have touched upon a sore point, Ibby, that Western journalists only now feel free to write about. With a strong bias towards the Bush and Blair policies on Iraq, the West saw the conflict in pure Anglo-American terms. However, those days have gone. Even after the formulation of the UN Coalition the efforts of the Arab states were never globally recognised or appreciated. It is absolutely true to say that without the logistical and operational assistance given by the Arab states, the speedy downfall of Saddam would not have occurred."

Mark was reinforcing Ibrahim's view that collectively the Arab states had given their full weight to the downfall of Hussein. Arab nations all along the Gulf including Kuwait of course, Bahrain, Qatar, the UAE and Oman, permitted US and British forces access and gave them storage and logistic support. Whether American, British or other nations, access would have demanded top-level talks and an 'access agreement' to be signed; all of these were honoured. Without the Arabian spring-board available to external forces, air operations, particularly the no-fly zone and force personnel build-up, would not have materialised.

"The good word of a Muslim can be traced back in history a long way," continued an aggrieved Ibrahim, "even the most difficult decisions have been addressed and agreed. You may not remember the case in 1699, right at the end of the 17th century, when Shari'a law was abandoned as a rule of external relations in favour of secular international law by the Ottoman Empire at the Congress of Carlowitz when the

Sultan agreed to a peace treaty with the Hapsburg Empire and the Venetian Republic? This was an extraordinary concession; Britain and Holland presided as mediators."

"Yes Ibby, I am not aware of that case but," pursued Mark, "the most remarkable of agreements reached in the Arab world at that time was that by the then King Hussein who not only had strong ties with the West but also had to meet the fiercely pro-Palestinian feelings of his people; he signed the Jordanian–Israeli Peace Agreement with Rabin at the Wadi Araba border post in the Arava Desert in October 1994. You will remember, Ibby, that this peace treaty was announced earlier, in July 1994, in Washington DC. It was also a success for Clinton whose backing underpinned the whole process you will recall. In fact Clinton stepped beyond the feelings of many of his Jewish lobbyists."

"Yes, and since then Mark, the Jordanians have maintained an unbelievable level of peace. On the broader picture in our Muslim world, across the globe since, we have signed countless agreements and stood by them. And most recently the world has seen how the Emirates have sponsored the America's Cup in Yachting. Sport sponsorship is one more of the very best ways of communicating to the masses that our word is our bond. We have given a breath of fresh air too, Mark, to the airline industry as well. In promoting openness to the world surely now it must be obvious that nearly all Muslim countries in the world are allies of the West or are friendly to the West?"

"Certainly, Ibby, no-one would deny your assessment. What we have today is a hang-over of deep-seated resentment and ethnic prejudice. Biased opinions based on insufficient knowledge are a common weakness in society; 'to jump to the wrong conclusion' is all too easy and is obvious."

"I guess so, Mark, but it hurts."

"Yes. I often think, Ibby, among the adult population of England immediately after the close of World War II, a similar level of bitterness and resentment of the Germans prevailed in my father's age group. But the youth of Germany turned that animosity around within a couple of decades and elevated their homeland towards a new plateau of understanding and real friendship with the English. I remember as a teenager visiting Germany and the common observation was that my German peers knew nothing of the War, didn't want to know anything of the War, and were heading in only one direction: *forward!*"

"Today we see just how successful that reversal has been, Mark. The Germans have the lion's share of the industrial growth of Europe on their doorstep. So perhaps we can learn from this, Mark."

"Yes, I believe so. The Arab strategy should be to bypass the present generation who participated in the Gulf War and concentrate upon the global integration of your children's age group who have the future to develop harmoniously." This was an important point being made by Mark who had every faith in the strength of up and coming generations of youth. Among them not only would new blood emerge but new and revitalised thinking on old problems would grace the world stage. Advances in computer literacy had generated global communications on a scale previously unimagined and as the computer was largely the tool of modern youth the boundaries of knowledge and research were being stretched in all the sciences. Mark continued optimistically: "You may not recall, Ibby, the words of one of the greatest of the Greek philosophers …… ."

"You know my classical education was limited to Islamic studies, Mark."

"Yes, Ibby. It was Aristotle, a pupil of Plato, and founder of the Peripatetic School, who once said: *teaching is the highest form of understanding.*'

"I read what you are saying, Mark and I have always said that 'education is the key' and still believe that, but perhaps we should refocus on how we teach, how we educate our youth and put the 'spin' on their education in such a way as to embrace their brothers around the world."

"Encouragement of the extensive use of exchange programmes at school and church, coupled with youth holiday packages on a 'home-swap' among families basis, will begin to create that footpath over the bridge."

"And knock down the walls of ignorance, talking of which, Mark, what was Aristotle's Peripatetic School?"

"The word comes naturally from the Greek, *peri*, about and *patein*, to walk. It was Aristotle's system of philosophy. He taught as he walked with his students around the covered walk of the Lyceum. This colonnade was called the *peripatos*."

"How amazing, Mark. He exercised and educated simultaneously!"

"Yes, and as we travel we learn; this holiday is a modern Peripatetic School for your youngsters!"

"Well, Ibby, we have a visit to a farm, today, and when that is over I really want you and the family to come and visit my own humble home, please?"

"We are looking forward to both, Mark, and it will be great to get out in the countryside without having heavy weather protection gear!"

"It can get chilly in Marlborough, Ibby, but the weather is distinctly warmer up here than down in Queenstown. I have some winter oranges growing and in fruit right now."

With slippery roads experienced over the hills from Blenheim to Nelson the family's vehicles advanced upon one of New Zealand's top operating mixed farms sheltered in the rolling hill, back-country, of a small rural community near Nelson. Mark had lived in that city once; it was a cathedral city, the tenth largest in New Zealand with a population of about 55,000 people. The region thrived on agricultural support for the all important farming fraternity and the loggers of the vast timber growing sector, and out at sea too, was a very active fishing industry centred on the Port of Nelson. Indeed the whole area was a pocket of paradise in the top northwest corner of the South Island.

A two-hour drive saw the family being met at the farm and it wasn't long before the ladies had taken a rest in the sumptuous lounge of the homestead while the men of the party had driven their vehicles in low 4 wheel drive up and over the rolling boundary lines of the estate. It was one of those perfect days in beautiful sunshine for which Nelson was well known. Perhaps it was a pity to be here when the golden to white beaches of the Abel Tasman National Park with magnificent marine reserves and coastal scenery was not too distant, but that was a summer activity.

"We have two thousand acres contained within 80 kms of fences," began the manager. "We carry about 4,500 sheep and 300 cattle. Our sheep are a successful cross of Romney, Poll Dorset and East Friesian and the cattle are a composite breed of mainly Angus, Simmental and Hereford with Charolia used as a terminal sire. We have a six-bay workshop and implement shed, a wool-shed and covering yards, lock up storage and a deer shed."

"But I don't see any deer," prompted Khamis to which there was a smile and a laugh.

"No. I don't like those deer and they don't like me!" the manager exclaimed. "We prefer to keep to the traditional stock of harmless sheep and cattle." Clearly handling deer was not to everyone's taste!

It was like a 'foreign language' listening to the manager as he continued to explain rotational cropping, how he deployed the stock and how with 14 reservoirs, 82 troughs, 25–30 km of piping and 25 storage tanks the water and irrigation system was kept going. His enthusiasm never waned and everyone learned that the sheep when fat enough would go to the local market and the cattle to Canterbury and Wellington.

It was an intensive programme and a busy life: January to March of each year saw the shearing and dipping of the ewes, the female sheep; the sowing of new grass and shearing of the two-year old sheep; and running the rams, the stud sheep, with the ewes in preparation for lambing, the birth of the new ones. Then the next quarter of the year, April to June, the calves were weaned; the rams removed from the ewes; the ewes sheared and their pregnancy testing had begun. Lambing and calving would be well underway in the third quarter of the year plus the shearing of the hoggets, the 12 month-old sheep, and the docking, removal, of the lambs' tails. Finally, in the last quarter from October to December, the sowing of summer food crops and shearing of the ewes, was followed by the drafting of lambs weighing over 35 kg and getting them to the market. December saw the weaning and shearing of lambs and hay making and if that was not enough, throughout the year was all the ongoing maintenance tasks of drenching stock against potential pests, eradication of weeds and mending of the fences.

Before their departure, the manager gave Ibrahim and Juma hands-on experience in the wool shed of holding the shearer's clippers in action, fortunately without the sheep! It was valuable educational exposure to what made one sector of the farming industry tick in New Zealand. After all, this was the mainstay of the country's economy and the backbone of livelihoods.

Havelock, a very small village but with a very big reputation, was the closest centre to Mark's home. It was the mussel capital of New Zealand for here was the focal point of a growing multi-million dollar industry in mussel farming within the sheltered waters of the Marlborough Sounds. Not only was Havelock the home of the delectable mussel but also was the school in which Ernest Rutherford received his early education. Rutherford (1871–1937), the son of a Scottish immigrant farmer, was the 'father' of nuclear physics who became world famous for his work in converting nitrogen to oxygen, and in splitting the atom, and then went on to develop the first nuclear weapons. It seems paradoxical and somewhat odd today that the nation which gave this man his education has declared itself to be nuclear-free!

As for the lowly 'mussel' these bivalve molluscs, which filter-feed on plankton and microscopic sea creatures, grew here suspended on ropes buoyed to the surface of the sea in the sheltered and inconspicuous bays of the Sounds. These waters provided some of the cleanest and most nutrient-rich, sub-tidal and inter-tidal conditions anywhere in New Zealand. Not surprisingly then the Green-shell variety of mussel, the largest of the species, grew undisturbed up to 240 mm in length. Mark's property, a small waterfront promontory, overlooked the principal navigable channel, Mahau Sound, along which the mussel boats would come into Havelock, the processing centre. 'Mahau' it was explained, meant 'safe' and indeed the interlocking waterways, between the undulating hills which made up the Sounds, did stretch out to the ocean and Cook's Strait. With his Scottish heritage, Mark had named his hillside home "The Kyle", which was Gaelic for 'narrow channel' or 'Sound'.

"When the skies are grey and the colours merge into all shades to black, Ibby," this spot reminds me of the Kyle of Lochalsh in the Western Highlands of Scotland. It is a very precious place for me albeit off the beaten track and remote from any sizeable town."

"Picton and Blenheim, I guess, will be your nearest major centres?"

"Yes, both have airstrips and if I really had to get to Wellington in the North Island I could be there under two hours routinely, and in only half an hour if the float plane picked me up off the waters' edge at the bottom of the garden."

It was a wonderful spot and as the sun had begun to set Mark offered the use and beauty of his home as a setting for their prayers, Maghrib. Windows faced due north, and from an external wooden deck with a glass-panelled balustrade, unrestricted panoramic views were afforded of this uniquely sheltered part of the Sounds. It was a fitting place of solitude for their Salat, the performance of Islamic prayer.

That evening, before returning to accommodation in Blenheim, Ibrahim and his family and Mark enjoyed the freshest of mussels imaginable in the tiniest of cafés in the centre of Havelock, "The Mussel Pot".

7

Wellington – Democracy Examined

"It is the largest wooden building in the Southern Hemisphere," announced Mark proudly as he pointed to the Government Buildings on the opposite side of the road to the Parliament Buildings and the Beehive where they were headed for an escorted tour.

"When I arrived here as a lad of 19," Mark went on, "I actually worked in the old wooden buildings for the Department of Internal Affairs; it was my first job in New Zealand."

This amazing rectangular, four-storey wooden building even had large portal columns which appeared to the eye as made of stone but were in fact, wood. "The internal corridors were wide enough to drive a horse and cart through in the old days," mused Mark. "In fact, the building is the second largest wooden building in the world after the Todai-ji, in Nara, Japan."

Built originally in 1876 it now housed the Law School of the Victoria University campus.

"What is also very interesting," Mark was now speaking to Ibrahim, "all the land the building is on, and indeed all the land in front of the road we have just walked along, Lambton Quay, is reclaimed. The Quay, as the name suggests, was in fact the original waterfront at which the sailing ships of yesteryear actually berthed."

"So the land in Grey Street where our hotel is, was also reclaimed?"

"Yes. Also of note too, is that the sand on the semi-circular beach in front of Oriental Parade, the road lined with the great Norfolk pines along which you took the family for a walk, was sand brought to New Zealand from England as ballast in the sailing ships; it was a good swap, the ships carried our wheat grain back to the people of England! Without the tons of white sand I think all we would have is the grey to black gravel of our volcanic soils. You appreciate, Ibby, that the whole of New Zealand is one complex volcanic mass and Wellington is situated, like San Francisco, right on an earthquake fault line!"

"Well, perhaps it is well that we do not plan to stop too long," smiled and contemplated a more than happy Ibrahim.

"In the Parliament Buildings, you will see how the engineers have reinforced the foundations of the old sections of the stone structure to resist earthquakes and all new buildings in Wellington must comply with standards of construction to protect against some level of potential earthquake activity."

"I guess then, Mark, all your domestic housing is a bit like the Canadian homes and built of wood to withstand the earthquakes?"

"Definitely; most homes are wood-framed with a variety of weatherproof exterior cladding materials and you will see in the alpine areas complete villages built with solid logs. These have been found to withstand the extremes of the weather and the heavy snow loads. Our building standards are high and this is reflected in the cost, of course. As a result, more and more New Zealanders are finding it harder and harder to break into the housing market."

"This has become a world-wide trend, Mark. In the UK, young couples face years committed to rental accommodation."

Although in a fresh breeze, the family had enjoyed a smooth and uneventful ferry crossing of the Cook Strait. They had travelled with their two vehicles on the Inter-island Ferry, the *Kaitaki* – the Challenger, from Picton in the South Island to Wellington, the capital of New Zealand at the southern end of the North Island. A major part of their travels was over and now a week was reserved to enjoy the best of the North Island before departure, eventually, from Auckland.

It would have been an oversight if the family had not been through the Beehive and the Parliament Buildings, the seat of government in Wellington, on their visit to New Zealand and so an escorted tour was arranged. Mark had always had a soft spot for the capital and both his younger brother and nephew with their families resided and worked in the city. Mark had also pioneered the sport of hot air ballooning in New Zealand at one time in his now distant past and he was very proud of the fact that today he remained the only balloonist with his co-pilot to have made the crossing of the Cook Strait by this very frail means of aerial transport. Pitting himself and his balloon against the notoriously capricious winds of the Strait had been a major accomplishment. He had taken off from the Marlborough Sounds and landed in the hills just outside Wellington City; that was in the 1970s.

As for 'hot air' the cynics would say that there was always an oversupply of it in the political sector and particularly so in the Parliament Buildings! It was, however, a very well spoken lady tour guide who introduced first the Beehive, then the two older buildings, including the Parliamentary Library, to the family. The Library originally was completed in 1899 and had been fully restored more recently to reflect its original character and style. The main complex was known as Parliament House and had, as the principal feature, the Debating Chamber, a room similar to the House of Commons in Westminster. Here the Speaker controlled debate and was always correctly addressed as Madam Speaker; currently and most unusually in New Zealand's politics both the Prime Minister and the Speaker were women. The Beehive, the most modern addition, of circular rotunda shape, was conceived by the Scottish architect, Sir Basil Spence, as a rough sketch on the back of a dinner napkin in 1964 when dining with the then Sir Keith Holyoake, Prime Minister of that time. The ten-storey building, 72 metres in height, did resemble a 'beehive' and hence the nick-name and housed the offices of the Prime Minister and Cabinet.

"What most people do not know, Ibby," said Mark quietly, "is there is a bomb-proof mailing room at the rear!"

"Oh; I also couldn't help but notice the airline-type security arrangements on entry and the presence of security personnel on all the floors we walked around."

"Sadly, Ibby, these measures have become necessary. I do remember the days when we had just one elderly gentleman who stood at the main door and welcomed you in!"

"So are these measures a result of the Al-Qaeda threat?"

"No, Ibby, our security provisions here were introduced long before 2001. We do have our share of political fanatics and anarchists and it would only take one such maniac to do a lot of irreparable damage or take the life of a politician. Fortunately, so far, no-one has taken it upon himself to attack our Parliament, yet, and long may that situation prevail!"

The tour guide outlined the New Zealand electoral system which had changed from the typical Westminster style of 'first past the post,' to a relatively new type of representation which allowed the voice of the very minor parties to be represented and heard. New Zealand had adopted, largely from experience in Germany, a method known as the Mixed Member Proportional, MMP electoral system. This granted each voter two votes, a party vote, and an electoral vote. The party vote helped decide how many seats each party would get in Parliament. The electoral vote resolved who would become the represented, local Member of Parliament. In simple terms, there were 62 general, 7 Maori electoral seats and 51 seats allocated from party lists; a total of 120 seats. Additionally, there was not in New Zealand an Upper House like the House of Lords in Westminster. Each Parliamentary Bill went through Select Committee research and presentation, with 3 readings, before the vote in the House and final endorsement by the Governor General of New Zealand and implementation into law.

The role of the Governor General, the appointment of which remained popular in New Zealand, was a spill-over from the old colonial days when New Zealand was a colony, then a Dominion of Britain. Her Majesty Queen Elizabeth II remained Head of State and Queen of New Zealand.

"On this point, Ibby, New Zealanders and Australians generally are opposed. In the Australian Senate, in 1975, the conservative majority was alarmed by the government's financial mishandling to such an extent that their inability to run the country precipitated a constitutional crisis. The Prime Minister of that time was a Gough Whitlam and he and his government were dismissed by the Australian Governor General, Sir John Kerr; this was an unprecedented move in western political history. New elections were called and normality was restored. However, because of this 'interference' there is a strong lobby group in Australia who want to declare the nation a republic and do away with both the Governor General and the Queen as Head of State."

"But this has not had a roll-on effect in New Zealand, did you say?"

"No. We are much more in favour of the retention of the Governor General and the British monarchy. You will have come to appreciate that most of our early settlers, and many since, have strong links with the aristocracy and well established families in the UK. Our ties with Britain remain very strong. I, for one," went on a modest Mark, "have expressed my allegiance to Her Majesty the Queen and was granted, I am delighted to say, a personal Coat of Arms by the College of Arms in London many years ago."

"The Tour Guide mentioned 7 Maori seats?" questioned an interested Khamis, "How many Maoris are there here, Mark?"

"Well, Khamis, the whole Maori situation has long been a subject for debate in New Zealand and really only now are we getting a format in both politics and social conduct which is acceptable to both ethnic groups. We have 15 percent of our total population who, during the national Census, have declared themselves to be of this origin, albeit true-blooded Maoris are extremely rare as so much intermarriage has prevailed. Because of this total integration we do pride ourselves as a nation to have largely eliminated racial discrimination but we do have a Race Relations Commissioner to act as a continuing watch-dog."

"So do you speak Maori?" asked a curious young Juma.

"Well, no I don't but many New Zealanders do."

"So there are no laws that insist that you do?" Juma continued.

"Juma let me tell you a little about our Maoris in comparison with our original white settlers. The Maoris call us Pakeha," returned Mark, inspired by the young lad's thirst for knowledge. "By about 1800 there were only a handful of ships that brought about 50 Pakeha to New Zealand. Fifty years later this figure had exploded to about 60,000 and by 1901 there were over 700,000 Pakeha here which made up 94.4 percent of the population. During the same period, Western diseases uncommon to the Maori, plus high child mortality among them, and deaths due to war, saw by 1896 the number of Maori fall from over 200,000 in pre-Pakeha times to just over 40,000. So in less than 130 years the Maoris and their language went from being predominant to one that was barely heard. Coupled with this, as you will appreciate coming from Arabia, the English language was always seen as being very important.

"So about 30 years ago, only 5 percent of our Maori children could speak their mother-tongue. To protect the language, Juma, it was resolved in 1987 to enact The Maori Language Act. This declared 'Te Reo' Maori to be an official language useable in our law courts if found necessary and more importantly it was introduced in junior schools. The Act is not about people being forced to learn Maori. It is about every child in New Zealand being given the opportunity. Also we now have both radio and television channels dedicated to the Maori language. Today more than half of the Maori people can speak more than a few phrases of their language."

"I guess that is good," Juma reflected, "and we have seen Chinese and Japanese people here, so why the bi-cultural national label?"

"Many New Zealanders, particularly the Maoris, see our country as bi-cultural, Juma, but they are very wrong. Yes, we may have had a bi-cultural heritage once but even from the earliest days of our history the Chinese settled here and worked the gold mines. Since then our main source of immigrants has been from Europe and South Africa but we have always had a trickle from the Pacific Islands, the Orient and Indonesia, India and the Americas. Our so-called 'bi-cultural' state is a complete misconception, like so many of the misconceptions your father and I have discussed about Islam – our little New Zealand is a multi-cultural society!"

"You were talking to my father awhile ago," rejoined a curious young Juma enthusiastically, "about the Greek philosophers. I am very interested in this question of democracy and how it can or cannot relate to our part of the world. What did the Greeks have to say about democracy?"

"Well, Juma, it is important for you to know that the very word, *democracy,* is in fact Greek, *demos-kratia,* the rule of the people. So the first lesson perhaps is that our Greek philosophers made the distinction by saying that it was the 'rule of the people', not the method of how those people actually ruled. So the word has a broad literal meaning. What we really mean today, which is consistent with what the Greeks thought, is that the Head of State, the Sovereign, the Leader, call this post what you will, is in the hands of the people with the degree of power granted to the leader and exercised by the people directly or indirectly; hence a State so governed. The word *Democrats* which you will be aware of in American politics, was a term adopted by the French revolutionists to distinguish themselves from the *Aristocrats.*"

"So how," Juma asserted thoughtfully, "did the word Democrat get into the American politics?"

"It was the choice of word adopted by the early Southern States in America, Juma, at the time of the abolition of slavery. Now, as you know, it is a political party more of the left than the Republicans, the opposition party. But what we really mean by the word *people* in reference to democracy is the *common people,* a state or society characterised by recognition of equality of rights and privileges; political, social and legal equality. In other words, equal rights for all."

"Some of us are born more equal than others, Mark?"

"No, Juma, definitely not; all men are equal and should be treated as equal! Equality exists in birth. However, Juma, with talent and ability, coupled with opportunity, individuals rise to different levels of performance. How our lives develop is a personal issue and dependent upon circumstance. Pure democracy is based upon 'equality' but the actual level of 'equality' achieved is reflected in the capacity of each country to grow. This is very similar to that of man, on ability and performance. In England democracy is centuries old; in the Arabian Gulf your nations are very young and political development has only just begun. A nation like Russia has only just demolished its 'iron curtain' and crawled out of communism and stepped over the brink of economic bankruptcy into a new 'democratic' environment, but in no way can we say that Russian democracy is the image of any other nation; it is specific to Russia."

"So I guess God-given talent, opportunity and education determine how we become what we are? So how did America become a Superpower?"

"Simply put, Juma, the industrial power base, the 'engine room' of America is like an impregnable fortress. The strength of the American economy was founded upon the wise use of resources backed by advanced technology, and a century of political and economic stability. Today, you will find the US Dollar in the reserves of every bank in the world. This factor alone is indicative of the extent of American influence and the trust that others have in that nation. Built upon that global trust is a network of commerce and trade that embraces the lives and hopes of many."

"So should we be striving to use the American democratic system in the Arabian Gulf, after all we have the natural gift of oil as our economic resource base?"

"No, definitely not, as the American or European democratic systems would not work in the Arabian Gulf."

"Why?"

"Again, Juma, simply put, with Western democracy we also have the clip-on addition of an enormous burden of bureaucracy."

"Bureaucracy; is this something we don't want?"

"You certainly don't want it on the scale that it is in the West! American bureaucracy is like a giant spider's web with the White House at the centre, Juma. This is the machinery of government through democratic processes where everyone, or almost everyone, is heard and submissions and legal niceties are observed. This 'machinery' is chronically slow and its boundaries are seemingly limitless and wrapped up in what we call 'red tape'. The democratic process is active at every level from the man in the street to the President. In Arabia you have, as I have said, young countries the infrastructure of which needs to be created and developed swiftly in response to the rapid growth both in population and the directed use of that 'natural gift of oil' to which you referred, Juma."

"Yes, Mark. I see your point; we don't have the luxury of time to re-build our nations in Arabia. Our task is big and to put in place the roads and highways, the airports, the hospitals and the schools we do need fast-track solutions to overcome our problems."

"And you wouldn't be able to achieve rapid economic and domestic growth if you were hampered by cumbersome bureaucracy would you?" Mark emphasised pointedly.

Ibrahim laughed and looked at his much happier young son and added: "Now, Juma, you can see why the Chinese have been so successful with their Three Gorges Dam and redirecting the flow of the Yangtze River. They never had to put up with the type of bureaucracy of the West. They just made up their minds to get on with the job!" Turning to Mark, Ibrahim continued, refreshed:

"Just as you enjoy your democracy, Mark, again many people in the West see all Middle Eastern nations as 'despotic and dictatorial states'. Admittedly some leaders have done little to improve the Islamic image in the West but continue to conduct the management of their nations by consultation. More so now than ever I believe."

"While I do not agree with just a consultative process, Ibby, as it lacks the 'equality of man' element," observed Mark, "I can see its real value in Arabia."

"We call it the process of Shura, the meeting and discussion of topics, the majlis concept. Our leaders don't just sit in an ivory palace; they get up and go out into the desert and the countryside and meet the people on their home, tribal grounds and sit and talk in tents in very much a time-honoured and traditional way. Everything concerning the welfare and rule of the people is discussed. These discussions do not conflict with the principles of Islam and the teachings of Mohammed the Prophet as there is a clear line of distinction."

"In effect then, Ibby, 'democracy' in a different sense does apply in the majority of the Middle East and the Arab world in as much as the independent rulers, whether they be monarchs, sultans or inherited family, patrimonial, leaders do involve their subjects in wide discussion?"

"Yes, the popular misconception in the West is that all our leaders do is dictate! This is completely wrong. Furthermore, our leaders have shown great responsibility in distributing their oil-enriched wealth to their people, providing education, health and those infrastructure needs on a generous scale. Also they address, and I stress in concert with the widest discussion of the people, even the tougher economic issues as we know that oil wealth will not be with us for ever. In fact, Mark, I remember the words of King Hussein of Jordon who once said: *Democracy does not consist merely of institutions. It is a tradition and a way of life that characterises society.* Above all, Ibby, our bureaucracy is reduced to the absolute minimum with major projects being launched in months not years!"

"What you are saying, Ibby, is that 'one coat does not fit all' and the democratic process is harnessed and channelled in a different way, more suitable to one than another, in Arabia?"

As the group then walked back via their hotel, the fascination of a quick trip on the funicular railway up the hillside from Lambton Quay to an observation look-out overlooking the City took hold in their imagination. So the cable car had become the next priority of the day albeit the weather had deteriorated significantly; low cloud and a moist air prevailed. It wasn't long before Ibrahim had them all on board the quaint railway which passed over three short bridges and through three equally short tunnels on an incline of 1:5. It had been a part of Wellington since 1902 and once at the top of the track they had a weather-restricted view of the capital. Fortunately the strong to near gale-force winds for which Wellington was best noted did not arise on that day. On the way down, students from the Victoria University boarded the railway. It was their cheapest and most direct route to Wellington's inner city and the large Public Library, and their Law School in the old Government Buildings. Their state university was founded in 1897, just before the cable car was officially opened, and was named in honour of Queen Victoria on the occasion of her Diamond Jubilee. The main Kelburn Campus resided on six 'vertical' hillside acres covering tertiary education in the arts, sciences and commerce.

From that world of academia at 'Victoria', Ibrahim concluded his stop-over in Wellington with an all important educational visit to the national museum of New Zealand, Te Papa, on the waterfront just a few minutes walk from their hotel. Te Papa, which meant 'my place', was opened in 1998 and enjoyed a worldwide reputation for its fresh and bold, up-beat, approach with a large number of mechanical and computer-generated interactive displays. New Zealand's history and culture was spread with encyclopaedic attention to detail over five floors all of which were interlocked within a state-of-the-art earthquake-proof building. New Zealand, with this remarkable museum, had at last 'come of age' and no longer was the nation lost in the shadows of global isolation.

8

Rotorua – Westerners in Arabia

"Our Ottoman sultans loved this, Mark," said Ibrahim wearily with his head just above the surface of the steaming hot pool. "They inherited the public baths from Byzantium. It seems some of the ancient customs of the Muslim Turks never rubbed off, or perhaps more correctly – washed off, on their Arabian fellows as we do not have a similar tradition of public bathing in the Arabian Gulf."

"No, regrettably, you don't," murmured Mark in a low almost indistinct voice with his head nearly submerged beneath the black waters of the mineral hot spring. "In fact, it is strange that the practice hasn't been adopted as you do have natural thermal springs in Arabia and with your Islamic ablution ritual I would have thought that the great traditions of the Ottoman Empire would have spread to the Gulf?"

"Well, we both are Muslim but our tribal and ethnic origins, Turks and Arabs, are poles apart as you know; however, I love the hot springs here in Rotorua!"

"Aye, these thermal springs are beyond belief. Did you see the note at the door that said a Roman Catholic priest, a Father Mahoney, walked miles to camp beside a spring here which he found in 1878?"

"I saw it!" interjected young Juma, "They called it the Priest Spring but I haven't seen that particular spring yet. What I am surprised to see are so many Japanese here, Mark, aren't you?"

Both Ibrahim and Mark looked simultaneously at Juma in response and then read a similar expression of curiosity on Khamis' face in the soft patio light which surrounded the partially illuminated pools; it was late in the evening. Ibrahim and Mark knew in an instant that public bathing was totally alien to Juma and Khamis; they had much to see and learn of our small but complex world.

Mark began to explain: "From birth, Juma, the Japanese all washed in public baths, as having piped hot water to their homes was a luxury none but the very wealthiest could afford. In the early days whole families would bathe in mixed village baths but today they have separate facilities. It is still rare in the rural areas for hot water to be available in all households and the old tradition of public bathing is still common-place. Showering in the natural, which you have also just seen in the masculine world of the men's changing room, is equally a traditional, normal way of life."

"Yes, I was very surprised to see everyone next to nature," said a slightly bemused Juma smiling, "but my modesty wouldn't allow me to share their bravery!"

"Well they are not being brave, Juma. Western culture, and in this case, Oriental culture, sees no harm or barrier to this kind of openness in life. The Greeks then the Romans ritualised bathing as an art. When you go to England next, Juma, call in at the ancient Roman city of Bath and there you will see the remains of the Aquae Sulis, possibly one of the oldest public baths in European existence which clearly reflects how important it was socially to be in harmony both with nature and your fellow man. Sadly, those baths are no longer operable, Juma, but partic-ularly the mineral, thermal, hot springs of today are valued highly for their therapeutic relief to aching muscles, arthritis and rheumatism. Right now, after our trip from Wellington, I can assure you this therapy is doing my old bones and joints the world of good!"

"I see the temperature in the pools is controlled between 38 and 42°C, Mark. Does it get any hotter?"

"No, not in the public baths; tomorrow, Juma, we will go and see the thermal valley and the mud pools and geysers. That's where it is really hot! Our geothermal power plants harness steam and boiling liquid in excessive temperatures and generate a constant supply of cheap electricity for the national grid." Juma and Khamis would later learn that of New Zealand's 129 identified geothermal areas which stretched from the top to the bottom of the country, 14 were in the 70–140°C range, 7 were in the 140–220°C range and 15 exceeded 220°C, with some down-hole bore temperatures recorded up to 326°C.

♣ ♣ ♣ ♣

The weather not been good as they journeyed from Wellington to Rotorua and they could only imagine the peaks of Ruapehu and Tongariro hidden by low grey to black rain-bearing clouds. As they approached the Desert Road as New Zealanders called it, they saw a region not of sand and rock which would constitute a 'desert' in Arabian terms but a wind swept, harsh and unforgiving landscape of bleak tussock-grass country. It was an exclusive training area for the Army, a place most New Zealanders were happy for the military to occupy but not themselves as mere human mortals! The hostility of the scenery, however, rapidly changed as the party drove through to Turangi, the trout fishing capital of the world. Trout were introduced to the area in the 1860s when brown trout eggs were brought from Tasmania, previously taken from Britain. Then the party travelled on to the placid shores of Lake Taupo, the largest fresh water lake in Australasia. This lake of 616 square kilometres was large enough to house the whole of the island of Singapore! Late in the afternoon the lake had taken upon itself a scene of absolute serenity and beauty but Ibrahim elected to press on to his planned stop-over in Rotorua. Soon lush green fields and undulating countryside, stocked with cattle and sheep, replaced the severity of the mountains. There was also a distinct change in the air; it smelt of sulphur. Indeed steam vents rising out of the ground as if by magic confirmed they were not only in the geothermal area known geologically as the Taupo Volcanic Zone but also they were almost at the heart of Maori country; the home of some of the oldest of New Zealand's Maori tribal settlements. This area, of Rotorua and its environs, was the focal point of Maoridom steeped in a rich Pacific Island heritage.

Being impelled into new experiences was always a character trait of those who extended the boundaries of their knowledge. Khamis and Juma, like their parents and sisters were all modern adventurers otherwise they would not have been in New Zealand at all! Well it was here in Rotorua that their taste for something different would be pushed to the limit. Reflecting seriously upon his own very conservative upbringing, compared with the extrovert and almost unrestrained licence he had given his own growing family, Ibrahim chatted to Mark.

"One of the problems with the people of the West, Mark, is that they seem to have this infallible belief that they are somewhat superior to the rest of the people on the globe. My children will tackle anything that their peers in the West can dream up; indeed for them every new idea from the I-Phone to putting a man on Mars is something to be tackled and addressed."

"Well, Ibby," remarked a quietly presuming Mark, "if by the West you really mean America with its meteoric rise as a superpower, I can understand why a feeling of inferiority can prevail among others."

"All men are equal, Mark," said a consolatory Ibrahim. "In the eyes of Allah we are all his children. Sadly in our world we don't all have the monetary wealth of others but what each and every one of us has is the inner quality of being the same. We are all equal."

"You are right, Ibby. Many writers have identified this air of superiority as a problem with the West. The arrogance in the West and the attitude of superiority serves only to inflame nations like Iran that almost certainly one day will declare that it has successfully tested a nuclear device with the full intention of using it militarily."

"The big hurdle we face every day, Mark, is that our children feel this inferiority thing and we must overcome it. I have even seen that many of my Arabian people are turning inward, turning a blind eye to the advances and customs of the West, and burying themselves in their Islamic past rather than meeting the challenge of the West, not half way but head on! What are we doing wrong, Mark? You know we tolerate Western culture with our expatriate community in the Middle East. In all but a few Middle Eastern countries, they are an integral part of the fabric of our society. We do not block their celebrations of Christmas and the New Year. In fact, quite the contrary; many Arab employers give expatriates both Christian public holidays and also those of Islam. We put up with their occasional lapses of drunkenness; we do not oppose their consumption of alcohol; we welcome their churches; we allow them their cultural nights, like the Scottish Burns' night and the Irish night; indeed we permit them in Arabia to live their lives as normally as they would in their own homelands."

"Ibby, I don't think you are doing anything wrong," rejoined a very serious, Mark, "what we are seeing is the American psyche in action. Here in New Zealand we have always lived under a similar cloud of inferiority with our big brother Australia on our doorstep, whose national mentality is to throw their perceived weight of superiority around. We clip their wings regularly in competition. Our All Black rugby team has knocked the socks of the Australians since time immemorial."

"So do you think it is just a question of competition?"

"Yes and no, Ibby; it is not that we do not recognise and appreciate the great achievements of the American people, we do; without the

American contribution to the globe we would all be worse off! But if the Americans were not a world superpower perhaps they would be more inclined to pay their full dues to the United Nations rather that sit in criticism of it? Perhaps too, if the Russians were the leaders in space, then a slice of American arrogance would disappear? It is interesting to observe, Ibby, that the British do not have this inferiority complex."

"Possibly, Mark, because every so often the British have led in such fields as industrial research and development. There are real brains in Britain plus it is a small country with a punch far greater than its weight. I am deeply aware too, that Britain is the nearest thing to a true multi-racial and cosmopolitan society. Racism and discrimination, particularly according to colour, is almost non-existent."

"I thank you for that, Ibby. You may like a view-point on race, taught to me by my father: he said that the people of the world were like the piano; there were black and white notes and when played separately they had nothing but a basic tune but when these notes were played together, true harmony was achievable."

"That was a nice thought, Mark. You must have had a very under-standing father?"

"Well yes, I guess so, Ibby. Certainly he had seen enough of the world to know that issues of superiority and inferiority were only a thin veneer. Looking over at the Orient, Ibby, and far into the future how should we view the new China? I have always seen China not only as a country but also as a civilisation. They have a heritage second to none and I am sure they do not have a feeling of inferiority, not even now?"

While many an economist had often voiced the demise of the great American industrial base, the collective economies of America and Europe with high standards of living were seen as the counterbalance to any economic challenge from a new China. However, it was a reality that the Asian powerhouse was one that America, Europe, Japan and an expanding India and South-east Asia would have to come to terms with eventually. Tables may not be turned but certainly the game of musical chairs would have to be relearned.

"Ibby," continued Mark positively, "your success in the future is to bring the word and wisdom of Islam to a religiously fractured and increasingly sceptical world that will find it more and more important to understand their neighbours. Your people, with your distinguished history of the sciences and medicine, coupled with your unrelenting belief in Islam with a tradition rooted so very firmly in the pages of the past, you have everything to be proud of and nothing to be ashamed of as we move forward. I often think of the words of Sir Peter Ustinov, an English-born writer whose father was of Russian and German heritage and his mother of Russian, French and Italian ancestry, who said: 'The world is my home and all the people in it are my brothers.' He meant those words, Ibby. As I have travelled around our small globe everyone I have met, from the Tibetans of the Himalayas to the Indians of South America, one thing is for real: we *are* all equal!"

"Well," announced Khamis breaking the deep thoughts of his father and Mark, "we are going to become extreme skydivers!"

"And Zorbanauts!" added a beaming Juma. "This place of Rotorua is a fun-filled place."

"Well let us go and see the Te Pui Thermal Village first," motioned one of the girls, "then you can do what you like!"

Jokingly with a wide smile Khamis said, "I have read somewhere that Rotorua is called the Sulphur City and Rottenrua!"

"As that may well be, Khamis," Mona cautiously added, "we are going to respect the Maoris and their lovely city; I like this place."

The wide, flat, open streets with trees planted everywhere coupled with period and decorative buildings with a large number of multi-cultural restaurants beckoned the traveller, albeit steam could be seen coming from under the streets and through storm water drains. Yes, the sulphur dioxide gas gave the city that sense of being in a pan of rotten eggs but it was a 'spice' of life not even the best of Indian curries could replicate.

Te Pui proved to be all that the guide books said of it, with bubbling mud pools, effervescent geysers and pumice rock of myriad volcanic colours. Of real value was a walk through the purpose-built, deliberately poorly lit, Kiwi House where three real little nocturnal kiwis pecked their way amid their bush surroundings. The 'kiwi' of course was the national icon.

"Perhaps," remarked Mark humorously, "the real human Kiwi should take a leaf out of its book: the kiwi is one of the only birds to mate for life and doesn't take another partner!"

"I am sorry to learn that the female egg is so disproportionately large," said a shy Zamzam, "it must make laying quite an ordeal for the female."

"Even more so, Zamzam, when the male fails to discharge his responsibility and walks away rather than incubate that egg!"

They all laughed; yes, Rotorua was a fun-filled city and quite different from the extreme adventure-seeking theme of Queenstown. It was a different world up here with the Maoris and as if to confirm this view the mid-day cultural show by the village Maoris was an excellent theatrical display. Everyone could not help but become a 'Maori' as they travelled through a timeless heritage lost among songs, poi dances, weaponry and stick dances, and the ferociously performed haka, the war challenge.

With a 'challenge' at the forefront of their minds, that afternoon the party went to the site of the Agradome not to see the sheep on trial but to join in two new and exciting activities. Extreme skydiving was the first challenge to be faced and the girls and Juma launched off on this literally hair-raising activity, one which required them to be suspended above a forced air current that supported their body weight. Exciting indeed to be free flying just a metre from the rubber platform but if that was not enough, other members of the family braved the impossible odds of surviving the Zorb. This most novel creation was a large double-skinned plastic ball with a hole in the centre just large enough to accommodate two or three human beings, 'zorbanauts', whose hapless destiny was to be released, stripped to shorts and singlet, saturated in a pool of water that remained with them as they were then rolled down a hill to tumble, tumble, tumble, head over heels! If one could imagine being the clothes in a front-loading washing machine, all that was missing in the Zorb, to simulate such an event, was the washing powder! It was a real human experience in bonding plus the greatest laugh imaginable; no wonder this activity was at the top of the 'must do' popularity poll in New Zealand.

"Sadly, Ibby, not all that glistens is gold in Rotorua. With its population of over 60,000 there are some disturbing and adverse social issues among our Maori people here, particularly among the lower socio-economic group. Severe criticism from all New Zealanders, including the Maori elite, recently has forced urgent legislation through Parliament to introduce the Child Discipline Act, 2007. Acknowledged by leaders of the Maori, the problem is essentially a Maori one. It is the question of child abuse on a scale otherwise never conceived in New Zealand. The absence of parental responsibility has forced the hand of the nation to legally step into the homes of the people and direct what is not acceptable behaviour."

"That is revolutionary, Mark."

"Yes, death after death has been recorded recently of lovely children who have been simply thrashed and beaten by adults so much that their short and precious lives have all too soon come to a premature end. As you can see, the Maoris and Pacific islanders are big people and a smack from one of them on a child is like a sledge hammer finding its target. Supervision of children has also been wanting. There was a tragic and recent case in a public park of an Island two-year old who was savagely mauled by a dog that ripped at the child's head as if it were a doll! The little girl was saved only by a passerby; the incident revealed that the child was not under any adult supervision at all!"

"Much of the problem has been placed at the door of the extended family concept of Whanau (pronounced: far-now) in which the care and custody of children is spread widely among many family members who have little to no direct interest in the welfare or development of others' children. Abrogation of parental protection and responsibility is something the wider New Zealand community just will not accept and I know too, that everyone in Arabia would share that view. Respect for offspring is something that our Maori and Island community has now been required by law to meaningfully address."

9

Waitomo Caves – Oil and New Zealand Horses

"Most people in the world simply do not understand the geography and politics of oil, Mark," said a quieter than normal Ibrahim as the day began. "Ignorance is rampant within the core of people who should know best and alarmist reports are both consistently inaccurate and commonplace."

"Well the alarmists of course link all Iraqi and Iranian politics to oil although common sense tells most people that a major slice of American politics is specifically geared to their ongoing quest to maintain their economic and hegemonic controls around the world, the oil factor just being a part of that picture."

"And yet, Mark, understanding that picture is relatively simple. Most oil analysts agree with the findings of the US Geological Survey which predicts that the peak in recoverable oil production will not come until between 2037 and mid century."

"So we have no grounds for fear that oil will cease to be available round the corner?"

"Absolutely not; and furthermore the Arab nations are deeply aware of their responsibility in producing oil at a rate their customers seek it, in the West and the Orient. More importantly, that responsibility extends to our belief that we make this major contribution to economic global prosperity sincerely; we don't want wars or a depression."

"I think, Ibby, much of the problem rests not in the understanding of supply but in coming to grips with the price. We have seen long queues at petrol pumps and meteoric hikes in a litre of gas."

"We will never see or allow a return to the oil crisis of 1973, Mark. That was a disastrous year for all concerned. Today we can more accurately foresee how economies are affected by winter and summer and the demands are much more measurable in the capacity of developed industries to actually produce goods. So although the demand for oil is constantly changing we can make better estimates, albeit our ability to

[61]

do so is compounded by variable stock levels held around the world and the ability of nations to ship and refine the oil. Although many predictions and assessments are made, demand levels do remain unfortunately as fluid as the oil itself. So the price gyrations we see directly reflect the market situation; some people make a profitable living being the 'fortune teller' on the oil price to the world and the International Energy Agency (IEA), the watchdog for oil-consuming countries, can only be wise after the event! What we have to do as producers is anticipate the future, react today and deliver tomorrow!"

Rain dispersed to give way to beautiful sunny conditions throughout the whole of the Waikato area through which Ibrahim and his family travelled during the day. They were in some of the wealthiest dairy producing farmland of New Zealand known as the King Country. Dairy products of milk and its associated items made up a third of the country's commodity exports. Many believed, incorrectly, that New Zealand's biggest overseas market was the UK. In fact it was one of the smallest with only 4.7% market share; China had 5.1%; Japan 10.6%; US 14.1% and Australia 21.4%. Interestingly, Australia generally was New Zealand's largest importer of all goods, regardless of type. Today, the undulating fields, hedge-rows and scattered trees of the King Country displayed a close likeness to the countryside around Cambridgeshire in England. It was no wonder that the first substantial market town they passed through was called Cambridge, the 'Town of Trees and Champions.'

Here, coupled with the dairying, the bloodstock industry was the finest in the land. Horses were raised, trained and sold on the world market; many to Arab nationals, particularly from the Arabian Gulf. In addition to the Gulf, buyers of horses were attracted from Australia, Hong Kong, Japan, Korea, Singapore, Malaysia, South Africa, Ireland, the Philippines, Macau, the UK and the USA. Bloodstock included weanlings, yearlings, two-year olds, tried and untried horses, broodmares and stallions. The 2007 New Zealand Bloodstock National Yearling Sales saw a new all-time high with a combined turnover of NZ$81.3 million, up a massive 24% from the 2006 figure of NZ$65.7 million, with the studs of Cambridge producing some of the finest horses of which the multiple champion Australasian sire 'Sir Tristram' and the current-day champion sire 'Zabeel' were just two.

"We actually have the New Zealand Arab Horse Breeders Society registered and well established here, Ibby, and we do compete, even in Arabia, the UAE in particular, with our Arab horses. Of course we export them too."

"Yes, I heard you have good Arab horses here, Mark. How do you ensure you keep a pure breed?"

"Well I am not a specialist in this field, Ibby, but DNA samples are taken and checked against the thoroughbred lines and this is a minimum for proof of export."

"Mark, I think we 'exported' the Arab horse first," joined in Khamis: "You will remember at the time of the Crusades we had our illustrious Muslim sultan Saladin who came to power in Syria?"

"Yes?"

"Well he is said to have sent to Richard the Lion Heart, when Richard lost his horse, a new horse because he thought such a brave warrior as Richard should not fight on foot!"

"I had not heard that before, Khamis, but now I am sure you know the ending of the Crusades?"

"Why yes, of course. It was our Saladin who united the Muslims and drove the Crusaders out, back to Europe."

"That goes to show, not only were the horses good in those days, Khamis, but so was the strength of Saladin's army."

"Although we won those battles, Mark, and the Holy Land was under Muslim administration for over five centuries we always allowed the Christian pilgrims to visit and perform their religious rites," clarified a concerned Khamis knowledgably who then added, "you also appreciate Mark, that we consider Jerusalem the third-holiest city in Islam, after Mecca and Medina?"

"Yes, I appreciate the distinction, Khamis. It is the long-term future of Jerusalem however, that is the political hot-spot in our modern times. What the world must bring to the table once and for all is that Jerusalem is the property of all the religions that claim it, not the sole property of Israel."

"For the Israelis, Mark," rejoined an interested Ibrahim, "the 'Wailing Wall' is the only tangible relic of their ancient kingdom of

Israel. At this place of prayer and sometimes with painful memories of their past, hence the 'wailing', Jews had met for centuries. But our tradition is that our Prophet Mohammed one night ascended to heaven from an outcrop near the Wall now graced by the Dome of the Rock. We also believe that it was Mohammed's holy horse that had been tethered to the Wall itself and above the Wall we have our Al-Aqsa mosque. So the stories of our Arabian horses go back to the Prophet Mohammed, himself." It was a warm and interesting discussion between Mark, Ibrahim and Khamis and as the day drew on, for every horse that appeared in a field thereafter, Mark wondered, if only these horses could speak!

Jerusalem was precious to all three of the great Middle Eastern religions; Judaism, Christianity and Islam.

Judaism was founded based upon the words of the Book of Deuteronomy from which it was believed that they were the chosen people. Also a part of their believed covenant with God was that they were given a 'promised land' with Jerusalem its sacred capital; that was Israel. However, for centuries few Jews had lived in the 'promised land' as most had been dispersed, hence the Diaspora, many to pockets within Europe and to a lesser extent the Middle East. By the 19th century, many in the Roman Catholic Church had condemned the Jews as the people who had killed Jesus Christ and later both the Catholics and the Orthodox Church blamed the Jews again, this time for conspiring to bring about the excesses of the French Revolution. Anti-semitism then nationalism – Zionism, emerged as time advanced and finally, by 1945, the Jewish people were determined to 'return' to the biblical lands of their perceived origin.

Christianity, on the other hand, was formed on the belief that in Jesus Christ a redeemer had been found. Eventually adopted by the Roman Empire, Christianity spread much more widely than Judaism. The basic tenets of Christianity were to love God and love your neighbour as yourself. With such an abstract foundation wide interpretation followed; those who followed the Pope in Rome separated from the Orthodox Church centred in Constantinople, then the Orthodox Church split between Greek and Russian components, then the Roman

Church into Catholics and Protestants. Other divisions also occurred, like the Coptic Christians and the Maronites, then if all that was not enough, the Protestants to this day continued to split into a myriad of sects.

Islam, which literally meant 'surrender' to Allah, was the successor to both Judaism and Christianity and inherited aspects of both. Islam was founded upon the belief that the Prophet Mohammed had received God's word as it was delivered to him via the Angel Gabriel and hence the profession of faith: 'There is no God but God; Mohammed is the prophet of God.' The Qur'an, related by Mohammed, was further supported by the traditions revealed in the Hadith, both of which were today the basis of the Islamic faith which gave emphasis on the community – the essential equality of all believers and the need to support the poor.

Jerusalem remained a holy city for all these three religions and furthermore, and much more significantly, Islam had pronounced and demonstrated throughout its history that it not only respected the faiths of Judaism and Christianity but also, being a related ideology that fitted into a tight chronology with these two other religions, it had shared many of their characteristics. Judaism and Christianity therefore had a special status within Islam and as Mohammed had acquaintances of both, Muslims were always taught to respect the other 'People of the Book'.

The peaceful flat to rolling countryside had given way in part to patches of primeval, native bush which had not changed since time immemorial. The whole of the land would once have been covered similarly but with man's thirst for property and later its development into income earning soil, the native bush was cut back and eventually receded. However, one untouched 'patch' became preserved for posterity. In 1887, a local Maori, Chief Tane Tinorau and an English surveyor, Fred Mace, when they were working in the area, came upon a cave at the entry of which led a stream into the bowels of the earth. That same entry point today was the doorway to the unbelievable Waitomo Caves. Unlike their Chief, who used candles and a flaxen raft to drift along the water course within the cave, his descendants today had developed a network of passages among glistening stalactites and 'mites to meet up with an engineless boat. In almost total darkness and silence, an absolute necessity, visitors then progressed underground to see upon the mud roof of the cave thousands upon thousands of unmistakably almost microscopic luminescent lights. The ceiling had lit up like a gigantic pin cushion with heads not of pins but more reminiscent of diamonds, that flickered and 'glowed' in their own image. These were the amazing glow-worms, *arachnocampa luminosa,* unique to New Zealand. It was a fitting close to a wonderful day and the return through Te Kuiti and the forest country reaffirmed the beauty of this central region of the North Island of New Zealand. Again that evening, the men indulged themselves for the last time in the hot, thermal springs of Rotorua while the ladies retained the select privacy of their Arabian modesty and went shopping, again!

10

Auckland – Arabs in Western Universities

Heavy rain had pounded the vehicles as they approached the city centre on the Southern Motorway from Rotorua to Auckland. Seemingly also with the intensity of the rainfall, every motorist appeared to be in an irresistible hurry to go somewhere! The roads were jammed packed with cars, trucks and motorway 'mad-hatters'! Ibrahim and his family had arrived finally in Auckland, the commercial capital of New Zealand. Gone were the placid days of driving through rural wonderland. Interrupted by the constant sweep of windscreen wipers, all the eye could trace now was a spider's web of roads, rail, roof-tops and rain, and more rain. Flooding had been widespread in the north and the east of the North Island but this was winter. The weather certainly did not appear to impact upon the Aucklanders' relentless enthusiasm and energy. This was one city on the move, day and night; 24-7.

After the family had located and moved into their hotel on the Princes Wharf, right in the heart of the CBD, Ibrahim and Mark had a chance to plan the few valuable remaining days and hours ahead before, regrettably, Ibrahim and family would return to their homeland in the Arabian Gulf. At a glance the guide books said it was a city of 1.3 million people and the largest in New Zealand. One-third of the nation's total population lived and worked in the Auckland region. Four 'cities' – Auckland, North Shore, Manukau and Waitakere – actually made up that region with three harbours, two mountain ranges, 48 volcanic cones, more than 50 small islands dotted about the Hauraki Gulf and countless golf courses, sporting facilities and rugby fields! In fact the guide books were quite naturally biased and endless with their praise for the place which New Zealanders viewed as the pivotal hub of their nation.

"I notice you have a good university here, Mark?"

"Two, in fact Ibby; the one you are looking at, on your map, is New Zealand's leading research-led university with over 40,000 students and by far the largest in the country."

"And the other?" questioned Ibby.

"AUT; you will see the signs around the city: it means the Auckland University of Technology. The larger university was established right from the outset as a university in 1883 but the AUT was our earliest technical college way back in 1895 and only became, in 2000, a full university. Both enjoy having overseas students from all over the world, of course. I am sure too, you will have some of your own nationals studying very hard here as well!"

"Yes, I guess so, Mark, our youngsters are all over the world albeit we have good universities of our own in the Middle East. Having our Arab students in Western universities surely is a great measure of our admiration and trust in Western nations and their cultures, don't you think?"

"Yes, trust on that scale is honourable in any man. You are very brave with that trust too, Ibby. Brave in the sense that your youngsters are given the freedom to become a part of the wider global citizenry in times when a conflict of cultures is a reality and an ever present threat to the personal safety of the individual."

"Students, fortunately, Mark, have always been free-wheelers and thinkers the world over and society respects their occasional periods of harmless rebelliousness and they become 'hardened' to criticism pretty quickly."

"Auckland certainly surrenders its Queen Street to demonstrations and to their eventual graduation parades. It is all part of the picture of life here in this very cosmopolitan 'circus', Ibby."

"Circus, it may be, Mark, but I am beginning to like the place and understand why so many of your Kiwis embrace its dynamic spirit. It is totally different, almost a world away, from the conservative and straight-laced Christchurch. By the way we must go to the Metro, I have been told it is unique?"

"It will be a first for me, Ibby. The Metro wasn't built when I was here last; I see it is a part of the Skycity operation, too. The family *must* go to the Sky Tower but let us leave that until tomorrow."

That evening the family walked for the first time along Queen Street, Auckland's principal shopping centre and main thoroughfare. The street was going through a major beautification programme which would transform the CBD into one of the world's most dynamic business and cultural centres. All this was a part of a much wider NZ$134 million, ten-year programme of infrastructure upgrade within the heart of the city. The Metro proved to be as exciting as expected with its futuristic and innovative design, cinema complex, gaming arcades, and multi-cultural restaurants. At the old Civic Theatre the family was also able to see a flash-back of three early promotional documentaries, *This is New Zealand,* as the New Zealand Film Festival was currently running; the theatre was packed. Like the cinemas, the public libraries, the parks, the gymnasia, the football fields, the athletics tracks and above all the ever visible water were all vitally important to the well-being and fitness of the citizens. Apart from the national game of rugby to which the whole nation was geared to seeing their All Blacks win cup after cup, the 'water' perhaps polled at the top of the recreational list. Auckland internationally was known as the City of Sails. Here was the home of the Emirates New Zealand America's Cup Team which had registered its intention to once again challenge the Swiss Alinghi at the 33rd America's Cup at Valencia in 2009. To see the water Ibrahim took the family over to Devonport on the North Shore by the Fullers Ferry. Mark pointed out how the Tank Farm, unmistakeably visible, was also a part of a much bigger 20–25 year rejuvenation plan called the Sea + City Project. The tanks would be relocated and Aucklanders would get what they had been asking for; a centrepiece of new green parks, increased public access to the water's edge, an urban village complex of shops, boulevards, apartments and restaurants. It was a multi-million dollar cooperative waterfront investment objective in line with the economic and social goals of the city. Mark wondered what the founding fathers, the 500 Scottish settlers who landed in 1842 on board the two ships 'Jane Gifford' and 'Duchess of Argyle', would now think if they saw their Auckland of today?

"As you can see, Ibby, the level of investment here in Auckland is almost exponential. When I see all this I often would like to just pop back to Oman and relive some of my most pleasurable times wandering around the Souqs of Muttrah where I could inhale all the scents and aromas of the spices and fragrances of incense; there is absolutely nothing like that here in Auckland."

"Well you cannot have everything, Mark! You will have to be

satisfied with the shopping malls and the concrete towers and glass buildings! Oh, and by the way just who is doing all the investing in Auckland, do you know, Mark?"

"Like any big city, Ibby, development funds do come from overseas investors but the bulk of the development continues to come from New Zealanders themselves. Almost all the new apartment blocks, and there are more and more being built now in Auckland, are financed by individuals as we have a system of granting freehold land titles for each unit within a large building block. Developers launch the projects then hand over the ownership and management to corporate bodies which themselves are controlled by the unit owners. It is fair to add, though, Ibby, that in Auckland specifically the Chinese immigrants to New Zealand have tended to congregate here although they are sprinkled throughout the country. With the closure of Hong Kong much of the wealth moved to Vancouver in Canada, Australia and thankfully, New Zealand. So we do have in Auckland some very wealthy Chinese Hong Kong exiles who have taken up residence and citizenship here. They have been welcomed of course and although you might find it strange, they all seem to have got the same idea and many have become our real-estate agents!"

"I haven't seen any China Towns on our trip, Mark. Is there any particular reason for that?"

"You will see collections of Chinese-owned shops in close proximity to one another occasionally, but you are right, we do not have China Towns or Greek or Italian or any other racially dominant and identifiable areas. We did have once, in a suburb called Howick, so many Chinese residents that it was nick-named 'Chowick', but those days have long gone and the Chinese have dispersed throughout the whole of Auckland. Answering your question, Ibby, the contributory reason is that our governments have actively encouraged all immigrants to fully integrate within the Kiwi character of the nation. What is pleasing today is that our Chinese people along with so many other Europeans and others do support both commerce and the public service; you will see the Chinese holding positions of responsibility in the Police, Customs, Inland Revenue and the Armed Forces."

"So are there any governmental controls on overseas investors?"

"As you would expect, Ibby, the answer is yes! Because we have to be sensitive towards land rights and claims lodged or concluded by our

Maoris, not all land is freely available in general. We have an Overseas Investment Office which receives all applications from interested overseas investors. The threefold objectives of this office are to ensure that no New Zealander is disadvantaged, that money-laundering is not permitted and that with any investment this would generate work for New Zealanders. Are you thinking of investing here, Ibby?"

"Well, many Arab nationals already have poured money into New Zealand, the bloodstock industry is one we have already discussed and we do like to keep our eyes open, Mark!"

"So your Islamic beliefs are not opposed to the principals of capitalism, then, Ibby?"

"That is another misconception of the Arabs in the West, Mark. Islam has never objected to capital investment. We have joint ventures and investment in industry globally. This is considered lawful. We have an 'enlightened' form of capitalism, Mark."

"So are you taxed?"

"What Islam has consistently been opposed to is your principle in the West of 'usury' where capital gains are made exclusively on interest bearing income. Interest-earning is against our Islamic belief but investment is not. You will recall Khamis briefly mentioned to you earlier our Five Pillars of Islam, the third of which we call *zakat*. This is our system of charity. Whereas capitalism is built upon a system of usury, and the Marxist and Communist socialism was one of abolition of private property, Islam has its system of social solidarity with mutually acceptable obligations and security within the community. Those who are more fortunate than others give in some way a part of their wealth to the poor. In your world you pay taxes to sustain your welfare state with so many cents in the dollar going to the State. We have a similar system of the rich giving to the poor and we prefer to do this in a manner that does not embarrass those less fortunate; we help with the development of homes and education. You know, Mark, in Catholicism that avarice and gluttony are among the Seven Deadly Sins and we, in Islam, do not countenance greed either. Depending on the level of our personal wealth we comply with the Third Pillar of Islam and proportionately give our zakat to charity as required. It is also important, Mark, to appreciate that an individual in the period of his actual life time is really only the custodian of his capital investments; families for generations thereafter are all beneficiaries. Above all, Mark, we pay God back by doing His work in the world and moreover, the greatest work we can do in His name is to give relief to suffering."

It was a perfect day, all the rain of the previous day had gone. There was not a cloud in the sky and the sun shone as brightly as it ever had done before. Today was the day when the family would visit the tallest 'ten-year old' in Auckland, taller indeed than Khamis! Built at a cost of NZ$75 million over a three-year period a decade ago, it was the Sky Tower. Some Aucklander, perhaps a drug addict, once described the tower as a 'giant hypodermic needle'! At 328 m the Sky Tower was the highest structure in the Southern Hemisphere and had attracted 1 in every 2 inbound international visitors to Auckland. Certainly the public gallery at the top was neither the place nor the time for either the drug addict or the faint hearted. With uninterrupted views for more than 80 kms the visitor could only but admire the brilliance of the engineers and the workers who had created this unique monument to modern technology. After a few moments of watching the bravest of individuals making the cable sky jump outside the window, Juma and Farah both unanimously decided that they were going to make this jump them-selves. With much discussion among the family Ibrahim had agreed and he, like everyone else, sat and waited spell-bound while Juma and Farah disappeared to Mission Control on Level 2.

It seemed like days as the family waited then the red illuminated sign above the window had flashed: 'Jumper in Five Minutes', then 'Jumper in Two Minutes', then 'Jumper in 30 seconds' and then as if by magic there appeared suspended on a cable outside the window, waving and smiling, a very excited Juma. Without warning he plummeted to the earth with the family and cameras watching every second of the drop; it was over! Over for one, that was, for his sister was next. The red sign seemed almost immediately to flash: 'Jumper in 30 Seconds' and sure enough clutching to her scarf in the fresh breeze, Farah appeared outside on the cable. Yes, she was smiling but the whole family felt for her as she too went plummeting to earth.

Unlike bungee jumping there was no hanging upside down or bouncing around, it was a controlled, swift cable release to a slower soft landing. Everyone returned to the base of the tower, down the elevator which seemed to fall at a similar speed as the sky-jumpers.

"So what was it like?' urged almost everyone with congratulations that had poured incessantly. Juma took up the challenge to reply, just as he had met the challenge to jump. Collecting his thoughts he methodically described his experience:

"My heart was pumping. After all I was about to jump the 192 m going at 85 kmph in 11 seconds to the ground below! Of course I was not jumping without safety equipment. There were three cables connected to my special 'Super Man' suit. I stood with Dave for a pre-flight photo and then I was ready to fly.

"This was the moment I'd been waiting for. I actually had dreamt several times of jumping from high altitudes without getting hurt of course. To make that dream come true, all I had to do was jump. So I counted in my head, 1, 2 and I jumped! I felt gravity pull me down but wait I was stopped, after just a few metres. Had it ended? Or was there a malfunction and had I to stop? I looked up and there was Dave clutching the camera. 'Just one more photo of you in mid air in front of your family,' he shouted. Directly in front of me was the window, the window you would have been behind. I couldn't see you but I imagined you all were laughing, some taking photos and a few praying to God that I wouldn't fall to my death.

"The photo only took a second and just as I looked at the ground below, I saw that at the spot where I was supposed to land there was a raised platform with a 'Bulls Eye' in the middle of it: I heard a click and 'wooohooo! I was falling with the wind in my hair, my arms and legs flailing, my heart still pounding and my mind racing. I did a series of moves while plummeting, like swimming, running and saluting the people below. When I touched the ground the third crew member disconnected the cables and loosened the suit for me. As I was seated, I waited to see the look on my sister's face when she also touched down."

"You are brave young lad, Juma," said a very proud father.

"And I think you have got guts and nerves of steel second to none!" added an astonished Mark. Then it was Farah who brought a touch of harsh reality to the drama of the moment.

"Well, I felt that signing the paper acknowledging my full awareness of the procedure was probably the craziest thing I have ever done and I don't mind admitting my legs trembled when I stepped out. When the lady told me to relax and enjoy the view, I couldn't, but I let go the handle bars and committed myself to destiny. It was one of those once-in-a-life-time experiences."

"I think you were wonderful, Farah," reassured her mother as her own pulse rate had now returned to normal. It would have seemed that the greatest concerns were held by those who never did the jump at all!

It may have been that this family had a 'death wish' for as they strolled down Victoria Street in the shadow of the Sky Tower they had come upon another adventure thrill seeker, the 3-seat twin tower bungee flight. Here three people were required to sit in parallel, strapped tightly to the chair and were then hoisted slowly upwards between two towers connected by long bungee cords. As the tension built up the release mechanism would then be activated and the occupants on the seat would be flung high in the sky spinning at least twice, like chickens on a spit would turn, before the cords would resettle and a return to earth was assured. Well, Mona, Zamzam and Rabab had a go at this aerial device but not without crowds of onlookers on the pavement building up to witness the event. Yes, they could all see that here were three traditionally dressed Arabian women taking a ride into the heavens. Just what were those spectators thinking? Ibrahim quietly whispered in Mark's ear, pointing to the increasing build-up in the crowd, "Perhaps they think a bomb is going to explode!" Certainly it was a public state-ment: Arab women were no different from anyone else, we were all equal in the eyes of Allah! For Khamis, he saw Mona, his 'Super Mum', propelled into orbit! He was deeply proud of her.

The last and singularly the most interesting of visits came just prior to the family's departure from Auckland International Airport. It was a visit to the Kelly Tarlton's Antarctic Encounter Underwater World. Here there were stingrays, sharks, octopuses, sea dragons, piranhas and a whole host of creatures from the depths of the sea all swimming in tanks and tunnels reflecting their natural habitats. But above all, the stars of the centre were the Gentoo and King Penguins in simulated Antarctic conditions; they were not stuffed but real, very real in a large quantity as a full breeding programme was in hand for these unique sea-birds of a wild continent in the Southern Hemisphere. It was the closest that most would ever get to a real penguin. Coupled with the snow-cat ride and a walk back in time through the replicated Captain Scott's hut, it would take little imagination to visualise how difficult it was for man to pit himself against the severe climate of that hostile continent. No wonder it was so sad that the bravery of those early explorers was met with such tragedy. Captain Oates' final words to Scott were now etched in history: as he stepped out into a blizzard he simply said, 'I am just going outside and may be some time.' None survived that expedition but we can now perhaps perceive more accurately, and realise more importantly, just how small had been the footprint of man in our wilderness of the Antarctic. The tour of this aquatic centre had transported Mark, Ibrahim and his family physically in time to yet another continent, indeed to another world. Humbled by the sheer majesty of nature, and knowing that the world we shared with these sea creatures had not changed for centuries, the experience had given this Arabian family a richer appreciation of God's Realm.

11

Reflections

———

"Well, Ibby, we have been talking together with your family, over the last few very valuable weeks, on a wide range of moral, political and religious feelings and matters, the very ethos of which is at the core of our own understanding and commitments to our faiths."

"Yes, Mark, and I hope the difference, indeed the divergence of our cultures is not so great as to create a chasm we cannot mutually bridge?"

"Well there is the simple question of who is an Arab and who is a Muslim; are they synonymous?"

"Mark by 'synonymous' I might begin to think you mean these two words have the same or similar meaning?"

"Clearly, they are different, Ibby?"

"Certainly they are, Mark, but are definitely related. An Arab is one of our race who has ethnically originated from Arabian soil and can normally read and write Arabic. Our heritage and rich history, of which I am very proud as you know, goes a long way back."

"You have every right to be so proud of such a wealthy heritage. We took your Arabic numerals and they are still very much a part of the English language and now a global business culture."

"A Muslim, however, Mark, as you do know is the follower of our Islamic faith which, like the Arabic numerals, is trans-global and Islam, his faith, is not constrained by geographical boundaries!"

"I had no doubts about the separate distinction, Ibby, but I raised the point with you merely to demonstrate how in the West such a misconception could easily arise. You may remember how our great historians used to talk about the Holy Roman Empire?"

"Yes?"

"Well that Empire was the confederation of Central European States that subsisted, either in fact or in theory, from AD 800, when Charlemagne was crowned Emperor of the West. That Empire in fact,

Ibby, remained outworn and dishonoured fiction until the early 1800s when Napoleon declared that the Holy Roman Empire was neither Holy, nor Roman, nor an Empire!"

"Precisely, Mark. That is why I am so concerned that the West today does not get hold of the wrong end of the stick concerning the Arab and Islam and place blame, particularly for terrorism, on the wrong doorstep! Much of the malicious content of the media and the misinformation fed to the public of the world does not attempt to make the distinction between race and creed, and from acts of terrorism and sectarian violence!"

"Confusion, founded upon ignorance, Ibby, is something we can only hope to reshape when fact is withdrawn from fiction and people are properly educated."

"Yes, Mark, this overriding business of re-education as the Chinese call it, is a major task and we must begin somewhere."

"Not in Re-Education Camps I would hope," surmised a jovially spoken Mark.

"No, Mark. Thank goodness we are not in China!"

On this point, Ibrahim and Mark were in unison of opinion and they would dwell upon the issue of better and wider education for months if not years ahead. For the moment, however, they were equally concerned on other points of pressing concern.

As their last full day in New Zealand together had drawn almost to a close, a studious and softly spoken Ibrahim broached a most penetrating question to Mark.

"As you know, Mark, as Arabs we place our Islamic faith uppermost in our lives. Islam to us is the basis of our daily way of life, it is the very foundation stone of our dealings in business and life, it is the moral code of conduct by which we operate, it is the guide to help us focus upon our duties within society and to help those less fortunate than ourselves. We demonstrate publicly, by openness of prayer, our total belief in Allah. We furthermore express our tolerance and understanding of the teachings of the Prophet Mohammed and endeavour to live our lives by the example he has taught us. Our commitment is life-long and our strength to continue through life is drawn from within the community of our Islamic leaders and from within the very core of our own family structures. These structures as I am sure you will appreciate are reliant upon the concept of the 'extended family'. In this we embrace old and young alike of several generations under the same roof and our cousins and their families are as one with each other." Ibrahim paused and added cautiously but directly: "Mark, how do you see the Christian way of life in today's modern society and how do you visualise the future of Christianity?"

Mark reflected upon the wisdom and the inner feelings expressed so succinctly by his long-time Arabian companion. Mark knew that a superficial answer would not be welcomed by this fellow professional whose whole life was dedicated not only to his faith and family but also to the unrelenting demands of investigative journalism. Journalism furthermore that was set in the theatre of Iraq and upon the platform of global terrorism. Every day, Ibrahim faced the challenge of survival both personal and psychological in the frenetic environment of death, disaster and destruction that prevailed in his beloved Arabia and elsewhere. His courage and his skilful continuity in the provision of unbiased and knowledgeable press and television reviews was basic to his own credibility in what was, after all, a cut-throat business, the business of reporting globally in the Information Age.

"Ibby, old friend," Mark began equally softly and rather uncharacteristically, very slowly, "in the West we clearly see how your Islamic brothers pay homage to their God. Our God also, I must add. The reverence you show outwardly without fear of hindrance is something too, that we can only but admire as your faithful have gathered over 14 centuries at the Hajj. They have made their way from every corner of the Earth on that pilgrimage to Mecca by every means of transport conceivable and the very fact that each and every one of you endeavours to make that journey at least once in your adult life is beyond the understanding of most within the West. To see your religious shrine and focal point of religious devotion, the *Ka'bah,* and the adjacent and magnificent building of the Masjid Al Haram, something we as Christians can only see on television, and for you to move among thousands upon thousands of like-minded pilgrims simply attired in your white *Ibram* garments, must be an experience for you, second to none in your entire life. You do know, Ibby, we have nothing in Christianity today, to compare with such an open demonstration of our faith."

"Yes, I am aware of that, Mark. About two-million converge on Mecca for about a week each year. It is the largest annual religious gathering in the world and I am proud of it."

"And so you should be, Ibby. Historically in the West we did have our pilgrimages: Walsingham and Canterbury in England; Fourviere, Puy, and St. Denis in France; Rome, Loretto and Assisi in Italy; Compostella, Guadalupe and Montserrat in Spain; Oetting, Zell, Cologne, Trier and Einsiedeln in Germany. But only on special occasions, and by tourists, are these places visited today in a similar way that if I was in Jerusalem tomorrow, I would immediately visit, of course, the Christian Church of the Holy Sepulchre. Ever since the 4th-century a church has been on that spot where the cave was, in which the body of Christ is still believed to have lain between His burial and resurrection. Similarly, if you visited Jerusalem I am sure you would stop-over at the Dome of the Rock and the Al-Aqsa Mosque?"

"Yes, Mark, and the Jewish visitors would stop at their Temple Mount and their Western Wall?"

"Yes, Ibby, but these are not pilgrimages in the sense of the Hajj." Mark paused then pressed on eagerly, "Christianity today, as it always has been for us, is based on Christ's two basic tenets: to love God, and love your neighbour as yourself. God Himself is perceived, not as of a human type, but as the embodiment of love. Christianity did accept, from Judaism, God's Ten Commandments but apart from these Christ did not set down a practical code for holy living. In this respect alone there is visibly a clear difference between the approach of Jesus and that of Mohammed. So for me as a Christian, Ibby, my approach is obviously going to be substantially different from that of your own way of religious life, albeit our two pathways ultimately lead to God.

"Globally, Christianity is very much alive. In the United States the Christian lobby is as powerful as the Jewish lobby in politics and almost all American families celebrate their Thanksgiving Day. Kiev is the cradle of Christianity in a much re-enlightened Ukraine, in the Lebanon you know just how significant the Christian view continues to be, and in China there is a marked swing from ancestral worship to Christianity, and above all, the Pope maintains a very active parochial watch over his Roman Catholic 'flock' across the globe.

"Many modern observers of Christianity believe our apparently weak structure has directly led to the downturn in numbers who attend our churches. It is also apparent, that 'being religious' is no longer fashionable in our information age of advances in computers and the sciences. With the exception of a handful of extreme sects, our main-stream congregations have diminished sharply in recent years with marriages and funerals being the main reasons to actually go to church. You will be aware, Ibby, of the empty pews in our western churches? You will be aware too that the numbers of people in the West who even admit to being of a Christian belief are also diminishing."

"Yes, I am aware of that, Mark."

"Recognising this problem is a real challenge, Ibby, but doing something to halt the downslide is something else!"

"Is this decline an indication of a lack of belief in the strength of your Christian faith?"

"There is an old proverb, Ibby, that states, 'the strength of the tree cannot be seen by its bark.' It is the view of many that what may appear on the surface does not necessarily imply or reflect what in fact prevails beneath that surface. Below that veneer of apparent indifference to religion, there is a very strong framework of Christian conscience within the West. We like to call this Christian awareness, the 'conscience of the community' with no direct appellation of the word 'Christian'. This conscience is in fact the quiet majority. For instance, our armed forces of both the United States and the United Kingdom are volunteer forces and both unstintingly have fought alongside your Arab brothers in Iraq and elsewhere. Human lives continue to be lost in what appears to be the cause more of others than their own. As the coffins of the dead soldiers return to their soils of origin in the West you will have noted that all receive both full military honours and a Christian burial. There is no greater gift than that of a life given that saves another. At the very root of that military commitment, albeit politically led, is the reality of a true Christian faith which demands that man must surmount evil. This inner human strength and motivation is borne through centuries of a heritage built upon conservative Christian values. Valour in the field of battle coupled with unquestioned devotion to duty is a derivative of Christian discipline. Only very recently, here in New Zealand, a young Maori soldier was awarded the Victoria Cross for his act of valour in the field in which he ran with his wounded buddy over his shoulders against enemy fire, in fact against the hostility of the Taliban resistance in Afghanistan. This is the strength of solid Christian belief.

"Our clergy do have a problem, admittedly, with being able to relate the concepts and terminology of the past to the present. For example, Ibby, you will appreciate that since the Reformation the English branch of the Protestant Church which, since 1532, has been known as the 'Established Church of England', because it was established by Act of Parliament, has disavowed the authority of the Pope in Rome and has rejected certain dogmas and rules of the Roman Church. It is these 'dogmas' that are difficult to translate into present-day life. More specifically, Ibby, we believe in the Trinity: the three persons in one God – God the Father, God the Son, and God the Holy Ghost. This ancient dogma almost defies translation into our modern society and our youngsters, quite naturally, simply are repelled by this mythological root; they do not have the knowledge or the patience to begin to understand. You will appreciate, Ibby that all our early mythology was based upon a threefold deity and a Trinity is by no means confined to our Christian creed. The Brahmins represent their god with three heads; the world was supposed by the ancients to be under the rule of three gods; Jupiter of heaven, Neptune of the sea, and Pluto of Hades. Jove is represented with three-forked lightning, Neptune with a trident, and Pluto with a three-headed dog! Furthermore the Christian graces are threefold; Faith, Hope and Charity. The Kingdoms of Nature are threefold; mineral, vegetable and animal. If all of this were not enough the cardinal colours are three in number – red, yellow and blue; and man himself is threefold – body, soul and spirit!

"Until fresh minds attempt within the Christian church to unravel the complex vocabulary of the past, we will continue to lose the adherence of our present and even future generations. The visible decline is disturbing but I do draw strength from those two basic tenets of Christ's teachings in the same way the Muslim is enriched by the word of Mohammed. We also have two very important prayers that reflect our Christian faith. The first you will be familiar with and begins: 'Our Father, who art in Heaven, Hallowed be thy name'; and the second, 'Teach us good Lord ………' It was this second prayer that Her Majesty the Queen recently used in one of her Christmas messages to the nation."

"Yes, I am familiar with the Lord's Prayer but I would be interested in hearing that second prayer, Mark, please?"

"Well, it is centuries old and goes like this:

'Teach us good Lord,
To serve thee as thou deservest,
To give, and not to count the cost,
To fight, and not to heed the wounds,
To toil, and not to seek for rest,
Save that of knowing that we will do thy will.'

"It is a simple prayer of Christian devotion to duty, Ibby, which we all learnt as children."

"Thank you, Mark. You are right it will be an enormous challenge for your theologians to retrace the past and bring it into the present. We must not forget that Rome was not built in a day!"

♣ ♣ ♣ ♣

"You will recall, Ibby that we have said that we both recognise and applaud the contribution that the United States has made and continues to make to our globe. Most travellers associate the statue of Liberty, at the entrance of New York Harbour, immediately with the freedom of the American people. Some also know that the statue in some way has reference to the commemoration of the American Declaration of Independence. Few today, however, know that the statue was presented by France to the people of America. So, even with this colossal copper clad statue standing as it has done since 1886, there is 'misconception' at least, as to its origin."

"Yes, Mark, it is all too easy in the rushed life-style of modern life to get hold of the wrong end of the stick."

"Purely by coincidence it was in the same year as I was born, that President Franklin D. Roosevelt went on record in a speech he made to Congress, on 6th January 1941, during the Second World War, when he said:

'We look forward to a world founded upon four human freedoms. The first is freedom of speech and expression everywhere in the world. The second is freedom of every person to worship God in his own way everywhere in the

world. The third is freedom from want……..everywhere in the world. The fourth is freedom from fear……..anywhere in the world.'

"I am sure you will agree, Ibby," Mark re-emphasised, "that this speech is relevant today?"

"Yes, the Speech is excellent and reflects an optimism which I also share. I live in hope that the people in the West, with wider knowledge and broader understanding, will come to fully respect my Arab nationals of today."

Epilogue

Brilliant lemon-yellow blossom of the wattle tree and the red and pink petals of camellia bushes heralded an early spring around Auckland. It was certainly warmer here in the north of New Zealand and despite all the gossip on climate change, Mother Nature certainly knew when one season was separated from another. For Ibrahim and his family the change in the weather was preparing them for the significantly hotter clime of the Middle East ahead; they shed layers of their thick clothing and became noticeably more at ease as the temperature began to rise. Auckland International Airport was an easy drive from the centre of the city and they could be certain that their Emirates Flight EK 433 would be on schedule as planned. It had been an action-packed holiday as intended with every day being fully committed. Their lengthy combination of return flights via Brisbane and Singapore would soon also be just another memory but for the hours ahead they would have that rare and pleasant opportunity of doing little else but reading, relaxing, eating and catching as much sleep as the flights would allow. Travel by air was always satisfying when trouble-free but all too often in this day and age the whole pantomime of security clearances, baggage checks and on-board procedures made flying just that little bit irksome.

Behind, they had bid farewell to Mark and Tony who would drive the vehicles all the way back to their origin at Christchurch and lastly, Mark would collect his own car and wend his way back to his retirement home in the Marlborough Sounds. For all, this adventure 'Down Under' had proved to be of lasting and significant value. For the youngsters they had been impelled into new experiences that would survive their lives and for Ibrahim and Mark time had 'stopped' just long enough for both to recharge the valuable memories they cherished. Before his departure, Ibrahim passed over to Mark two exceptionally interesting books: *The Prophet Muhammad*, a biography by Barnaby Rogerson, and *Muhammad, A Prophet For Our Time*, by Karen Armstrong.

♣ ♣ ♣ ♣

In the peaceful setting of his own home, Mark read first one then the other and followed up much of what was written by both Rogerson and Armstrong from within other references and works he possessed. The joy of these two books was that they were works on Islam written by Western authors and, more significantly, written in 2003 and 2006 respectively. This recent release propelled Mark more closely into the present without the distraction of obsolescent material. While Rogerson's work was a chronology of the Prophet's life in strict historical terms, and valuable for that reason alone, Armstrong's book provided an academic's philosophical view with expressed concerns for the future. Both were excellent. In expressing her concerns Karen Armstrong reiterated the findings of an eminent Canadian scholar, Wilfred Cantwell Smith, who observed in his book, *Islam in Modern History*, in 1957:

'*Unless Western civilization intellectually and socially, politically and economically, and the Christian church theologically, can learn to treat other men with fundamental respect, these two in their turn will have failed to come to terms with the actualities of the twentieth century. The problems raised in this are, of course, as profound as anything that we have touched on for Islam.*'

Karen concluded that: '*the brief history of the twenty-first century shows that neither side has mastered these lessons. If we are to avoid catastrophe, the Muslim and Western worlds must learn not merely to tolerate but appreciate one another.*'

However, since 1957 when Wilfred wrote, not only had half a century elapsed but also the world had seen a quantum leap in computer sciences with the knock-on effect of a dramatic swing of the pendulum in favour of previously disadvantaged nations. Fast-track implementation of 21st-century solutions was now a real option in dealing with old problems. The world was the recipient and beneficiary of the information age with even the remotest parts of the Congo, the Amazon and New Guinea having access to the television and the network of global communications. Talented individuals from even Third World countries had through their study and personal diligence risen to prominence; it was a different world.

Back in Iraq jubilation, not blood had poured onto the streets when the Iraqi national football team, the Lions of Two Rivers, beat the Saudis in the Asia Cup Final of July 2007. Sunni, Shi'a and Kurd players constituted the Iraqi team. Throughout the whole of Iraq thoughts of war and sectarian violence had evaporated, albeit momentarily. Was this not the real Islamic way, of peace and reconciliation?

Arab nationals for all of the 21st century had sent their sons and daughters to the colleges of knowledge in the West. Many of these youngsters had faced and met the challenge of cultural shock by actually living and boarding in the homes of European and American families as they progressed with their studies. But how many Western youth could say the same about experiencing some level of integration with their Arab peers in their homes in Arabia? With a touch of arrogance they would have said that: 'there was no need'. Reciprocity, that mutual exchange of privileges and advantages between countries, was more important today than ever before. Exchange students in Europe, America, China and Japan, and for the very few lucky youth of Arabian countries, had been successful but none of these had ever been on the same scale as the numbers of Arab students who now studied in the West. Somehow this imbalance deserved correction if the Western youth of tomorrow were to grow up with a clear knowledge of the customs of their equals in Arabia. With football being such a sensational social sporting activity perhaps a greater level of exchange between Junior Football Clubs, and indeed other sporting codes, should be encouraged with the 'host' being a home not a hotel, so that all players, supporters and fans could share a common cultural exchange experience. Recognising that education was really the single key to unlocking the frequent chasm between different nationals, the widest possible engagement and cross-pollination of cultures was seen to be the most optimistic avenue for future exploration. This was not new or revolutionary but should the peoples of the West engage more freely and honestly on Arabian soil, they would find that the Arab was a friend not foe.